UNEXPECTEDLY
HIS

A SMART CUPID STORY

MAGGIE
KELLEY

Entangled Publishing, LLC
2614 South Timberline Road
Suite 109
Fort Collins, CO 80525
Visit our website at www.entangledpublishing.com.

Lovestruck is an imprint of Entangled Publishing, LLC.

Edited by Vanessa Mitchell
Cover design by Heather Howland
Cover art from Shutterstock

Manufactured in the United States of America

First Edition August 2015

To my one and only.

Chapter One

"Gee, how long can I be sexy?"
—Marilyn Monroe

Marianne McBride sat inside the darkened cake, her serious, efficient brain full of second and third and fourth thoughts. She pressed her palms into the sides of the moving confection and drew in a deep Ujjayi breath. She should be at home, peacefully drinking Chardonnay, watching *The Seven Year Itch*, not freewheeling into a birthday party.

"Are you ready, M.A.?" asked Jane Wright, bestie, boss, woman at the helm of the cake. The dark-haired Mila Kunis look-alike wore a curve-hugging LBD and an encouraging smile. "All that time studying Marilyn, doing Zumba, shaking your groove thing is about to pay off."

Was she ready? Her heart was hammering so hard, she could hear it echoing against the interior walls of the flippin' cake. *What was she thinking? Exploring her inner siren!* She wasn't a siren. For heaven's sake, she'd blushed at the swimsuit issue of *Sports Illustrated* when she'd stumbled across it on her ex-fiancé's nightstand. *Exactly.* Her blush, his nightstand, and *Sports Illustrated* were only three of the reasons she'd agreed to strap on the ruby red heels. And not the most compelling reasons. She'd already spent too many sleepless nights analyzing her ex's claim that she was prudish and unadventurous in bed. Certainly pouring her curves into a silver-spangled burlesque costume and climbing into a birthday cake qualified as adventurous.

Another breath. "I'm ready, Jane. I can do this." Easy peasy, lemon squeezy. Just a step, a confidence-building excursion. "I *want* to do this."

"And you're sure, right?" Her friend's voice held a hint of uncharacteristic hesitation, and the cake rolled to a stop. "Because you're going to be amazing. Better than the actual cake girl."

The double-booking of the *actual* girl was the reason Marianne was tucked inside the cake. This was not her usual Friday night. But not one to change course once she'd processed the analytics—and statistically speaking, this particular venture should accelerate the process of liberating her inner siren by 42 percent, plus or minus a few percentage points—she adjusted the feathery mask she wore in place of her horn-rims and drew in one last fortifying breath. "I'm sure." Marianne closed the pop-out top.

And the cake began to roll.

As they moved from the back office toward the main bar, Jane nattered off a list of instructions and advice. "Take it slow—you don't want to trip over the edge of the first tier. Remember to breathe, smile…" More words filtered in through the papier-mâché walls. "Music…spotlight…glasses on the vanity." She tried to process them, but her practical brain had left the bar nineteen minutes and forty-two seconds ago.

Finally, the cake came to a stop, a bit like Marianne's heart, before it started pounding against her sequin-covered chest. She heard Charlie Goodman, owner of the bar and Jane's fiancé, step up to a microphone. "Tonight we've got a surprise for the man of the hour."

Oh God, she was starting to sweat. There was a loud click, and she felt the heat of a spotlight hit the cake. She drew in a breath as burlesque-style music burst from the sound system, its throbbing beat her cue to exit in a hail of tiny paper squares.

Inner siren, don't fail me now.

She burst out of the cake in one swift, just-close-your-eyes-and-do-it motion and the crowd in the dimly lit bar erupted in appreciative applause. Confetti flew everywhere, through the air, down the layers of the cake, into her cleavage. The rhythmic thump of the music seeped under her skin, boosting her confidence. Tomorrow, she'd happily welcome back plain, efficient Marianne. But tonight? Her inner seductress was tossing caution to the wind like confetti. This was her subway grate moment.

Her Marilyn moment.

As she shimmied over the rim and down to the second layer, her eyes scanned the crowd, hoping for a glimpse of the birthday bad boy, but without her glasses, she couldn't see past the last layer of the cake. Then a slow, measured movement at the blurred perimeter of the spotlight caught her attention.

Nick Wright.

He stood apart from the lively crowd, his hands buried deep in the pockets of his dark, sleek pants, and for a second, she literally stopped breathing. Behind the mask, her eyes drifted a shade lower. He was just…wow, the whole tall, dark, and handsome package, with a set of incredibly broad shoulders that made a girl feel like she could let down her walls and rely on him to hold her up.

She lifted her eyes to find his gaze settled on her. Looking at her the way he looked at her in her dreams. Eyes locked on Nick, she ignored the faint trembling at the edges of her body and focused on her instructions. *Settle onto the second tier, sing happy birthday, and blow a kiss into the audience. When you're finished, Charlie will roll you out of there.* Except now her arms were shaking. Not to mention her legs.

The room grew quiet, all attention focused on her as she moved to the next tier. She stumbled, briefly, a small mistake that she caught quickly enough to be sure no one had noticed. Perched safely on the second tier, she drew in a breath and started to sing in her best Marilyn. *Happy birthday to you…*

Even to her own ears her voice sounded breathless.

Nick stepped inside the circle of the spotlight. She blinked several times behind the mask. Maybe he couldn't hear her. As if pulled by some unknown gravitational force, her body unfolded from the second tier. Her hips adopted an unfamiliar bombshell kind of sway as she moved toward him, the spiked heels clicking against the tile floor. *Happy birthday to you.*

He was only a few inches away now, and in better focus.

A vaguely stunned look marked his face, which didn't say much for her cake jumping skills, but still, he was standing there. *Happy birthday, dear Nicholas.* She swayed closer.

His hand fastened to her hip, tugging her closer still. *Happy birthday to you.*

She could see him perfectly now, his midnight blue eyes, gazing down at her. Leaning forward on her ruby tiptoes, she pressed her lips against his in a kiss so sweet, Marianne thought her heart would melt like buttercream frosting. And she never indulged in buttercream frosting. Lost in the feel of him, her lips parted, unexpectedly deepening the kiss. She reached for his shoulder to steady herself, fisting the fabric of his shirt.

Hours ago, kissing Nick Wright had been a statistical impossibility, but now, here she was, holding him close, reveling in the bittersweet taste of his kiss. Her kiss.

Easing away, she gazed up into his handsome face, her tingling lips curving into a small smile. "Happy birthday," she whispered, turning on her stilettos to beeline past the cake.

Behind her, Marianne heard an outburst of cheers. A quick glance over her shoulder confirmed her suspicion that a small crowd had formed around Nick. She dashed into the storeroom. Jane's voice called after her, but she ignored it, embarrassed that she'd kissed her friend's brother. Her *boss's* brother. Kissing wasn't part of the deal. Leaving the second tier wasn't part of the deal. Maybe tomorrow she'd be able to face her bestie/boss, but tonight she was fleeing the scene, racing home to her moderate glass of wine — make that the bottle — and classic movie.

Tripping into the storeroom she kicked off the heels,

grabbed her Keds, and shoved her feet into the slip-on sneakers. She snatched up her everyday clothes, which she'd left in a neatly folded stack on a shelf, but there was no time to change. She needed to hurry out of here to catch the last cab before the midnight rates kicked in. An oddly pragmatic thought, she acknowledged, considering her getaway plans. Still, in the event that the birthday boy wanted to canoodle with the exotic cake girl, she needed to be gone. Exploring her adventurous side was fine, but Marianne had bumped up against her limits. Kiss or no kiss, she wasn't the confetti and cabaret type.

Where were her glasses? *Think, Marianne, think*. Jane's voice calling her name sent her into a second mini panic. She couldn't breathe. The darned spangly dress was so tight. Pulling at the top, she forced in a rush of air and retraced her steps. Where had she been when she'd tied on the mask? The mirror. The bathroom. She'd left her glasses on the vanity.

Her clothes tucked under one arm, Marianne rushed into the bathroom. She palmed the granite surface for her horn-rims and cursed the genes that combined to give her 20/200 vision. Dagnabbit, now was not the time to be functionally blind. When her fingers hit pay dirt in the form of a hard plastic lens, she practically cried in relief. She shoved the specs against the bridge of her nose, and everything snapped into focus. *Everything*. Her gaze locked onto her sparkly reflection in the mirror, her blue eyes bright, cheeks flushed pink, her cleavage spilling over the top of the silver dress. This was not her.

Kissing Nick had been a fantasy, a dream, but tomorrow she'd be the same old Marianne she'd been yesterday. The career-focused, nerdy girl with her nose aimed at a computer screen.

And he'd still be the bad boy with the quick wink and the devastating grin who had charmed the panties off half the single women in the greater metro area. A serial dater. A man whose relationship rules included no back-to-back dates and no Sundays during football season. Arrogant. Rude. Presumptuous. And so ridiculously sexy, she'd traded her cardi and capris for a dress straight out of a Kardashian's closet. *What had she been thinking?* For heaven's sake, she saw him every week at Smart Cupid and he still called her "New Girl". She'd shaken things up all right, but now, she needed to shake her tail away from the scene of the crime.

Bolting from the bathroom, she grabbed Jane's trench coat from the back of a random barstool and hurried to the exit as footsteps fell against the tiled hallway. At the back door, safe and unseen, she turned and caught a glimpse of Nick lifting the turquoise mask from the floor. His eyes scanned the empty room for a woman who was already long gone. A wave of sadness washed over her as she stood immobilized, her back pressed against the Art Deco building's brick wall, her unadventurous heart locked firmly back in its cage.

"Happy birthday, Nick," she whispered. And with her body still trembling, Marianne dashed to the curb to hail her midnight cab.

Chapter Two

"Manliness isn't always easy."
—mantelligence.com

As Nick Wright strode across the marble lobby of his firm's upscale Manhattan offices, the same damned question that had been on his mind all weekend long circled back around again. Who was that girl in the cake? Followed by a second question, why the hell did he care so much?

Sure, the girl Friday night had been a surprise. Strike that. Not a surprise. Nick had known he'd be taking one on the chin as soon as his future brother-in-law, Charlie Goodman, started hard-selling a birthday bash at Temptation.

After all, this was hardly his first rodeo. But the girl Friday night wasn't your average girl in a sequined dress and take-me-now heels. There was something else, something sweet and vulnerable about her—innocent, even. One look, and Nick had wanted to take off his carpincho jacket and wrap it around her silver-strap-covered shoulders. And when she'd stumbled, he felt...protective.

Not his usual reaction to a woman and not one he'd experience again if he could help it. Nick enjoyed being the guy taking off the jacket...slipping off the silky shirt...easing away the lacy panties. A new woman every other week worked just fine.

He was up-front and honest with every woman he took home. Commitment—out. All-night, pleading-for-more-sexy-times-between-the-sheets fun—in. Usually, he went all the way in...slow and deep and all the way in.

A smile pulled at the corner of Nick's mouth. A night or two playing "slow and deep" with his mask-wearing cake girl would be enough to dispel that nagging, wrap-her-in-a-protective-jacket-and-take-her-home feeling. He was sure of it. And damned if he didn't like a challenge, especially when it came packaged with curves. But since his wide-eyed mystery woman had made a run for it, Nick didn't expect to see her again. Given his long-standing commitment issues and occasionally less-than-stellar judgment—probably a good thing. He cruised down the professionally decorated hallway.

Outside his office, Nick's longtime admin looked up from the stack of paperwork threatening to overtake her desk. She was wearing her patented expression of disapproval, a harbinger for the rest of his day. He was pretty sure that if Peg hadn't logged in forty years with the firm, she'd have pronounced Nick too much trouble and taken an early retirement. Luckily, she had a soft spot for him. "Morning, Peg, you and your grandson enjoy the Yankees game this weekend?"

His assistant offered a smile. Her grandson was the key to her heart. "Loved it. Thank you for the tickets. Not every seven-year-old gets box seats and a chance to run the bases after the game." Nick nodded, pleased to hear the kid had enjoyed the game. Peg leaned closer, gestured toward his office and said, "Boss Man's been in there all morning waiting for you."

Nick rubbed the strung-out muscles at the back of his neck. Ever since the ex-wife of the firm's biggest client decided she wanted Nick to be her post-divorce Transition Man, he'd been in deep shit at the firm. She wasn't the first female client to try and catch Nick's eye, and he'd probably earned the shitstorm aiming for him like a category five hurricane. But that didn't mean he had to like it.

At least he'd enjoyed the ride. Several rides actually. Just none with this particular woman. Even Nick knew better than to play with that brand of feminine fire, but the client was calling for his head, and some of the partners at Morgan Wealth Management & Trust wanted to give it to him.

"Thanks for the heads-up, Peg." He pushed into his office. Behind the desk, Daniel Morgan sat facing the wall of windows that framed the city skyline. Nick suspected he wasn't here for the view.

"Nick, we've got a problem." Without turning, his boss cut straight to the chase. Direct, smart, and not a man to suffer fools, Dan was an old-school attorney who took both people and his business seriously. A collection of traits Nick admired. He swiveled around and looked him square in the eye. "Here's the deal, kid. Bill Jeffers wants your dick on a pike."

Nick winced and shoved his hands deep into his pockets.

"Sounds uncomfortable."

His boss didn't seem amused. "Listen, we both know you've steered clear of the man's wife. Wisely, I might add." Nick started to confirm, but his boss waved away the need for a response. "I like you, kid. I told Jeffers that. I told him I know for a fact you wouldn't go near his wife, but the man doesn't know you like I do. He said he doesn't trust an unmarried man. The situation is a tough one. Jeffers brings in big money. If you want a shot at the upcoming partnership, you need to clean up your act." Rising from the chair, he stepped out from behind the desk. "Fast enough to satisfy Bill Jeffers."

Nick wasn't big on ultimatums, but if securing a partnership with the city's most prestigious wealth management firm meant getting his shit together—he needed to do it. Being considered for a partner bid was an honor, albeit one he'd earned. He'd worked his ass off, but the credit crunch had not been kind to a number of private equity firms. Morgan had held strong, wisely muscling-up investment returns for their clients, but passing Nick over for a safer, less controversial choice would be easy. He was lucky to have Dan on his side. "I know how important reputation is in our business, and I appreciate the support. I'm willing to do whatever it takes to fix the situation and prove myself to the firm."

Dan walked toward him, stopping an arm's length away. "You know what I'd like to see you do? Settle down. Find some sweet woman who can keep you out of trouble while Jeffers has you in his sights."

He rolled back on his heels. "I could probably do that."

An image of a certain silver-spangled cake girl filled his thoughts, but he shoved the image aside. He needed a woman to keep him out of trouble, not consume his every waking thought.

"Probably?" his boss asked.

"Definitely," Nick said. All he needed to do was play his cards right with his matchmaking sister. "In fact, Friday night was my farewell to bachelorhood party."

Dan's eyebrows raised in anticipation of an explanation. Nick winced. Dammit, now he had a situation on his hands. He needed to come up with details—fast.

"A night on the town before my engagement."

"Your engagement?"

Oh shit, had he overstepped? An engagement? His collar tightened at the thought. He'd tried the relationship thing a few times in the past, but commitment led to pain. His parents' marriage had taught him that. Better not to be in a committed relationship than hurt a woman the way his father had destroyed his mother. And shit, now he'd gone and said the *E* word? An *engagement* might be tough to pull off. He'd really hung his balls out there.

"Nick?"

A thin film of sweat formed on the back of his neck. A partnership position at a high-flying firm like Morgan confirmed he'd made it out of Brooklyn. Hell, in the world of legal finance, he was about to make the NFL. A dream.

He needed to strike now or they'd move onto the next guy. Manhattan was full of sharks. He'd already given them reason to pass him over, and there was no guarantee the chance would come around again. If that meant he needed to find a sweet woman willing to tolerate him for the short-term...

"Dan, all that's left to do is get down on one knee,

propose, and convince her to say yes." Nick pressed his palm against the center of his chest. "What can I say? I fell damned hard...out of the blue...like being hit in the back of the head with a ball peen hammer." God, could he string together any more romantic clichés? His boss seemed to be Hoovering them up like candy.

Dan stepped forward, his hand extended in happy congratulations. "Welcome to the club, kid. I know just how you feel."

Poor bastard. I'll bet you do.

"Thank you, sir." Nick accepted the handshake with the straightforward strength of a man with nothing to hide. All he had to do now was find a woman.

Unfortunately, Cupid's arrow hadn't struck him yet.

Luckily, he had the queen of hearts in his back pocket.

"Jane, you are killing me here." In a casual move that belied the anxiety building in his gut, Nick kicked back on the velvet sofa in his sister's office. Apparently, producing a short-term fiancé in a matter of hours was not going to be as easy as he'd hoped. He was already going down in flames.

"Me? Killing you?" Jane rolled her eyes and rummaged through that alphabetized candy drawer of hers, not at all amused by his current dilemma. "I can't run through my database and magically hook you up with some temporary wife. My clients are looking for true love. You, big brother, are looking for a way from the doghouse to the executive washroom."

Nick groaned. Ever since she'd gotten together with

Charlie, she was all hearts and cupids. He almost liked her better when she was betting his friend's love life on national television. "C'mon, sis, I need a fiancée—stat—and since my newly committed-to-love sister is the city's smartest Cupid…" He tossed out the all-hands-on-deck smile that used to con her into doing his chores when they were kids. She'd do the dishes and he'd sneak off to meet some girl by the river. Worked every time.

Jane pulled two bags of Skittles from the drawer and backhanded a pack that hit him square in the chest. "Nicholas, I'm going to keep this simple for you. There's no way I'm setting you up with a client. Never going to happen, not in a million years."

Apparently, the smile didn't always work.

"So, I take it, that's a no?" He tossed the bag of fruit candies onto the sofa.

"Yes, that's a no." A quick tearing of candy wrapper emphasized her words. "Can't you seduce, or rather, convince one of your gal pals to sign on the dotted marital line? Jessica, for instance? Or what about that yoga instructor…what was her name…Dharma? Yes, Dharma would fit in very well at the firm."

"Give me a break, Jane. The women I date—"

"The word 'date' seems like a stretch here."

The muscles in his jaw clenched defensively. "We both know I'm not suited for lasting love, hell, I'm not suited for love of any kind. I enjoy my freedom, and while the women I date are varied and wonderful, I don't want one of them taking this engagement thing to heart and ending up with one that's broken. I'm not that guy. I'm easy, fun, sex-on-the-side guy."

"Oh, right, I forgot," she said with another eye roll. "Love's all about sex on the side."

"I think I liked you better before you became engaged to my best friend," he said. "Besides, I'm not talking about love. I'm talking about marriage."

"A fake marriage. No, wait a minute, that's a little heavy-handed on commitment." She sliced through the air with her hands in an emphatic gesture. "A fake engagement."

He ignored the sarcasm and got up to pace the floor in front of the oversized desk she used to intimidate people. "What about the girl from Friday night?" Nick stopped and ran a hand over his jaw. Damn, he hadn't meant to voice that particular thought. He turned toward his sister.

Her eyebrows rose, feigning disinterest. "You mean the girl from the cake?"

"Yes. The cake girl." His eyes narrowed on her face. What was with the sudden lack of interest? His phone pinged, but he ignored the incoming text. "I asked Charlie how to contact her, but he didn't have a clue." Another ping. Damn, that was getting annoying. "How the hell can he not know where to find her?"

"Booking agents are so discreet nowadays," she said, back to sarcasm and eyeing his phone. A third message lit up the screen. "Why don't you answer? Maybe one of your current 'first-date-with-benefits girls' would like to sign on for the long term."

Nick wagged a finger at her. "See? Now, that's what I was talking about. That's the kind of thinking that gets a man into trouble. I don't need a girlfriend, I need a fiancée." And then it hit him like an overwritten legal brief. "Or… maybe I need a professional." Maybe he hadn't thought it through until now—after all, what did he have to offer a woman looking for true love?—but a business relationship could definitely work.

"Really, Nick?" She raised an eyebrow at him. "A professional temporary fiancée?"

"Why not? All aboveboard, nobody gets hurt." He countered with a cool shrug, unwilling to be dissuaded from an idea that could save his ass. "Maybe even a professional cake girl, one willing to sign on the dotted line of a short-term business relationship."

"But as you've already said, we don't know how to find that girl." There was a thoughtful pause filled by the sound of Jane's fingers drumming across the desk. "However…if it's a strictly hands-off, business-type situation… I may know the perfect professional woman." Her shrewd, slightly devious gaze narrowed on his face. "What about Marianne?"

"The new girl?" Nick shook his head in an imperative no. He'd run into her at Smart Cupid once or twice. She was nice enough, but always reserved and blushing. In order to convince his managing partners he'd fallen madly in love, he'd have to turn her into the type of woman he'd be willing to fall madly in love with. And frankly, he wasn't sure it was possible. "There's no way in hell anyone will believe I fell head-over-heels for the buttoned-up new girl. The woman is so not my type."

Jane shot him a pointed look as another message hit his phone. "Apparently, your type hasn't gotten you very far. Maybe it's time to try someone different."

"Not that different." Nick powered down in order to avoid any more shit, wondering how the hell he'd managed to put his career in the love-thirsty hands of Smart Cupid.

Even the one he was related to, no strike that, *especially* the one he was related to.

"Nick, remember the decent, protective side of you. Remember that guy? The rock that held our family together after Dad lost his last bet, racked up a stack of bad debts, and took off. Why don't you try being that guy for a change?" His sister leaned forward, her elbows on the desk, a recognizable gleam in her eyes. He was going to pay for coming here. "Never know. Might improve your attitude about love."

Nick crossed his arms over his chest and let his silence speak for itself. Life had dealt them a lousy hand, and yes, he'd put school on hold to make some badly needed income for his family. He'd waited up for his mother to come home from her second job and watched out for Jane and Jake, making sure they never saw their father drunk enough to take his shit out on their mother. He'd do anything for his family. But he'd survived, hell, they'd all survived, no reason to dwell on it now.

Jane let go a sigh. "Fine, since you seem to need additional inspiration to make this work for you," she said, her expression telegraphing her irritation, "I happen to know she's in need of an escort…"

"An escort?" Even he was shocked.

"Not that kind of escort," she said, shaking her head like he'd lost his mind, "A date. For an important family…event."

"Jesus, not a wedding." Nothing worse than a damned wedding.

"No, Romeo, not a wedding…never mind, forget I said anything."

A charged silence filled the office. Nick turned his phone over in his hand a few times. She was playing him. He knew it, but he'd backed himself into a serious corner by claiming a fiancée he didn't have. He shoved the damn cell deep into the pocket of his pants, not believing what he was about to say. "Think she'd be willing to make a deal?"

"I think so," she said, all eagle-eyed. "If you'd be willing to help her out of her situation."

"Better not be anything illegal."

Jane laughed aloud. "No, counselor, she didn't do anything illegal. If you want to negotiate, she's spending her morning at the New York Sport Club. Better go over there now, so you can catch her before she finds another date." He opened his mouth to speak, but she waved him off. "Yes, I'll call ahead and plead your case."

He cruised over and planted a fast kiss on her cheek before hitting the exit. "Just make sure New Girl knows the relationship is all business."

"Be grateful. You'll be damned lucky if she agrees to this scheme of yours." Hustling out from behind the desk, she called to his retreating back. "And don't call her New Girl." He waved a hand in the air and kept walking as her voice leaped up an octave. "Seriously, Nick, if you hurt this girl, I will be forced to go all Don Corleone on your ass." At the sound of her palm hitting the doorjamb, a smile creased his face. "Remember the cannoli."

"Love you, Janey."

Nick turned to give his sister a wink. He was unafraid of her jabs about the cannoli. But he got the point. Assuming the new girl agreed to play fiancée, Nick's rules did not apply. He wasn't about to screw around with his sister's friend. This engagement was a totally hands-off situation, which was completely fine by him. He was growing tired of sleeping around. His phone always pinging. Feminine texts with emoticon hearts interrupting him at work. A new woman every other week had worked fine until a recent ex-hookup set him up with a fake Tinder account that sent his phone ringing off the hook. Yeah, a break from dating might be nice. And who knew? As long as there was no danger of commitment, this engagement deal could be a good thing, especially considering the women hassling him for promises and the bind his reputation had gotten him into at work. Yes, this could work, and despite the fact that New Girl was as far away from his type as a woman could get, he was already grateful to her for saving his ass.

Potentially saving his ass. If she agreed. *God, please let her agree.*

Only one issue left on the table. One possible glitch. He'd seen the scheming glint in his sister's eyes before she'd switched over into Mafia mode. Cupid had strapped on her wings. But if she thought for one second he was going to fall for her matchmaking tricks and ride off into the sunset with Little Miss Cardigan, well, she had another thing coming.

Nick Wright fell for no woman.

Chapter Three

"A wise girl kisses but doesn't love, listens but doesn't believe, and leaves before she is left."
—Marilyn Monroe

*D*ance it out, Marianne thought, swiveling her hips to the Latin rhythms emanating from the gym's built-in speakers. *Just dance it out.* From the back row of her third Zumba class, she followed the instructor's choreography with enough desperation to dispel her recent misguided mistakes. A memory-killing salsa move to the left, a hypnotic twist of merengue to the right. Throw in some "Jenny From the Block". *Dance that inner siren back to the grotto…turn the deadbolt…and cover it with duct tape. Lots and lots and lots of duct tape.* She rolled her hips forward. That darned siren was never coming out again.

Talk about a weekend of regret. Even thinking about kissing Nick near the blurred edge of the spotlight Friday night made her sweat-slicked skin burn with humiliation. All she'd wanted was a chance to test-drive her skills, but the whole siren thing worked better in theory than practice. A tiny crush was fine, but that kiss...that kiss never should have happened.

Nick Wright was everything she objected to in a man. Arrogant. Rude. Presumptuous. A sweet-talking man's man all dressed up in a mesmerizing package. She wasn't sure which was worse, the fact that she'd climbed into the cake or the fact that she'd run off as if the kiss had been more than a simple happy birthday.

Don't analyze. Just dance.

As if enough Zumba classes would erase the memory of Friday night. She closed her eyes and drew in a deep breath as the music slowed into cooldown. She'd taken the sequined getup to the dry cleaner and asked them to deliver it directly to Jane so she'd never have to see it again. As for facing Jane...well, Jane was her boss so she couldn't hide from her forever. She'd avoided her calls all weekend, but now that she'd taken the day off, Jane might get worried. Eventually, she'd have to explain the impromptu kiss and her panicked exit.

No sense overthinking the situation. She grabbed her water bottle and headed downstairs to shower and change. Best to simply put the weekend behind her, resume her normal life, and forget all about kissing Nick Wright. *Easy peasy.*

Once at her locker, she pulled out a fresh towel, her neatly organized toiletries, and her cell. Unsurprisingly, there were a few texts from her boss. She stabbed her rec specs against the bridge of her nose and opened the most recent message. *The answer to your homecoming prayers is waiting outside.* Cryptic, even for Jane.

Homecoming prayers? M.A. returned her towel and cosmetics bag to the tidy locker and closed it tight. *Was she talking about her dad's fresh-out-of-federal-prison party?* Yes, she'd mentioned needing a date, but Cupid wouldn't try her tricks on her. *Would she?* A nervous feeling settled in her stomach, and Marianne hurried up the stairs. She didn't like surprises, especially surprises that couldn't be managed or quantified, she thought, bursting out the front door of the gym. *Especially surprises that looked like Nick Wright.*

The breath rushed out of her body. What was he doing here? Besides leaning against the silver railing on the outskirts of the fountain, looking all self-assured and male in his to-die-for pinstripes and power tie. Egotistical. Overconfident.

So not her type.

Except that he was totally her type. Dark hair, cropped close, always perfectly neat. Blue eyes the color of a dark and stormy summer sky. And a stride as measured as a metronome.

He looked over and caught sight of her, his blue eyes narrowing as if he wasn't sure it was her. Not surprising. He'd never even looked at her before, not really. Mostly, he seemed to smile through her, always charming, always slightly distant. He eased away from the railing in a smooth move and walked toward her in that deliberate way of his.

A sudden tidal wave of panic rushed through her. Did he know she was the girl from the cake? Was that why he was here? Her humiliated heart beat wildly against the spandex, knowing she'd have to face him every week in the office. Hells bells, she'd kissed him. She'd have to quit her job and move to another state—no, another country—and she wasn't even very good with languages. She shook her head as if to clear away the panic. Jane wouldn't betray her confidence that way. But then, *why was he here?* He couldn't possibly be...her *date*? In his cool, even stride, he closed the distance between them. "Hello, Marianne."

Oh God. Oh God. Oh God. That voice. That deep, honeyed, ready-to-teach-a-buttoned-up-libido-a-thing-or-two *voice*. He was gorgeous, yes, but it was his voice that made her knees buckle. She wanted to hear him whispering sweet everythings in her ear. She'd had dreams about that voice. Late night dreams. "You called me Marianne."

Taller than her by a good six or seven inches, even with her one stair advantage, he gazed down at her. His perfect mouth curved into a playful smile. "That is your name, right?"

Marianne's face scrunched up behind the glasses. Had she fallen down the rabbit hole into an alternative universe? The easy manner. The smile. The teasing tone.

Was he flirting?

With her.

Outside New York Sport Club.

His gaze moved over her, taking in the daisy-covered halter and coordinated Spandex pants, practically burning a heated trail through the polyester-polyurethane copolymer. He was definitely flirting, and the look in his eye made her wish she was wearing her oversized college sweatshirt. Or a suit of armor. She wrapped her arms around her torso to hide the spandex and glanced down at her faux-camo sneakers.

"What do you say, Marianne?" he asked, in a playful tone that sounded as if he'd been calling her that forever.

"Will a six-week engagement work for you?"

Her eyes snapped to meet his. "An engagement?"

In her limited experience, men like Nick Wright rarely skulked around Zumba studios, flirting with women whose names they could scarcely remember, so the words "six-week engagement" left her a little confused.

From the look of him, Nick felt the same way. "Jane didn't tell you?"

Marianne blinked over at him from behind the glasses. "Tell me what?"

Nick ran a hand across his clean-shaven jaw as if he were about to broach a tricky subject. "No calls or messages, maybe a text?"

A text?

Her pathetic heart slammed into her chest so hard she could scarcely breathe. Had Jane told him about her dad's party? Was he supposed to be her date? A hot blush stained her cheeks. "A text? Um, no…well…yes."

Nick lowered his chin in a slow nod and waited intently for an answer. When none came, his dark brows rose as he asked, "Which is it? Yes or no?"

She blinked again. "To the engagement issue or the text question?"

Nick glanced around the stone plaza as if searching for an escape route. Not that she blamed him. She must look like a lunatic in her rec specs and Zumba gear.

"Is there some place we could go to get a cup of coffee?" he asked.

Definitely an alternative universe. Nick Wright asking her out for coffee. The idea that he might know about the cake resurfaced, but she shoved it aside. "I don't drink coffee."

"You don't drink coffee?" he said, rubbing his hands together. "Okay. Good to know. How about tea? Do you drink tea?"

"I drink green tea—and fruit smoothies."

"Green tea." He nodded. "Excellent. Can I buy you a cup of green tea or a smoothie?"

Marianne nodded, unable to stop the smile from spreading across her face at the thought of a mini date with Nick. "There's a juice bar inside. Will that work?"

"Let's hope so," he said, before throwing out that full-wattage smile, the same one he'd given her the first time she'd seen him, the one that had left her literally speechless.

The juice bar bustled with its usual crowd, young mothers whose kids were spending time in the gym's childcare facility while mom worked out, a few professionals logging workout time during their lunch hours, and a plethora of Manhattan cougars, all of whom had their not-so-discreet eyes aimed at Nick. His pinstriped suit stood out in the sea of bright, floral spandex, but that wasn't why they were looking. Nick stood out everywhere.

Marianne sipped her tall blueberry acai and tried to ignore the way their eyes locked onto Nick's spectacular backside as he walked toward the corner table where she sat quietly waiting. She tried not to worry about the disbelieving looks thrown in her direction, looks that said a woman like her failed to rate a man so flat-out delicious. Not that it mattered. Despite Friday night's birthday kiss, he didn't belong to her. The cougars were right. She didn't rate.

An especially pretty one gave him a come-hither smile and tossed Marianne a dismissive once-over that stung like a slap across the cheek. Nick turned away and settled his gaze on Marianne, giving her a lingering look that sent Come-Hither Smile slinking back to her coffee. Arrogant, yes. Presumptuous, absolutely. But he'd defended her, a fact that sent a thrill racing up her spine. He winked and folded his long body into the plastic chair across from her. *Eat your heart out, cougar.* Maybe she didn't rate, but right now, he was with her. Potentially hers for the next six weeks.

Marianne cleared her throat. "So, you need a fiancée?"

He flashed another of his charming, arrogant smiles and she practically melted into her smoothie. "And *you* need a date."

She did. She needed a date for the Martha-Stewart-on-steroids blowout her mom was planning to celebrate her father's freedom. Having supported her dad through the whole insider trading mess, her ex was sure to be there. If she intended to prove to his miserable cheating backside that she'd moved on, she needed a date. Preferably a hot date. Maybe a gorgeous Brooklyn date who smelled like freshly laundered Merino wool and Irish Spring, a combination that was knocking her hot pink Zumbas off. "I do. For a family event," she said, taking another sip of her drink in an effort to hide her nerves, "in the Hamptons."

The word "family" seemed to turn him green, but she crossed her fingers and ignored his typical male reaction. He cocked an eyebrow. "What kind of event?"

So he was an eyebrow cocker. She could handle it. "A private one."

Nick nodded, opened two creamers, and emptied them into his coffee. His whole demeanor was casual, but Marianne wasn't fooled. She suspected this was how he bested his opponents in negotiations. All casual and cool before he ripped them to shreds. "And how is it that a girl like you can't find a date to a party in the Hamptons?"

A girl like her. Casual Nick played hardball. Well, two could play that game.

A blush bloomed on her cheeks as she swirled the straw inside her cup in her own indifferent way. "How is it a man like you can't find a woman willing to marry him?"

He gave her a short nod at the evasion. Maybe she unraveled when it came to men, but she hadn't negotiated Wall Street deals for nothing. They both knew why Nick was more interested in a business arrangement than a real engagement. His reputation preceded him.

Nick sipped his coffee. "Some unexpected trouble at work…"

Her brows rose above the glasses. "Woman trouble?"

"Not of my own making," he said without missing a beat. "But, yes, woman trouble. Now if I want to win a partnership with the firm, a partnership I've earned, by the way, I need to come up with a fiancée. Preferably, a short-term fiancée."

Her lips rounded into a small circle. Typical. "This is all about a job?"

"Not a job, a partnership with the most influential firm in the city," he said, his still sexy tone decked out in irony. "If I were you, I wouldn't be so judgmental. An engagement seems like an extreme way to solve a party date issue." She wrinkled her nose. The man did have a point.

"What are the terms?" she asked, spitting out the words

before she changed her mind. "Of our potential six week engagement."

Nick leaned back in the plastic chair, his hands tented in front of him. "Ideally, you'd move into the condo this afternoon…"

Her eyes widened behind the glasses. Honestly, jumping out of his birthday cake was one thing, even pretending to be his fiancée. But living with the man? The thought of such close daily proximity to Nick Wright sent her senses reeling into next week. "Move in?" she asked, trying to keep her voice from rocketing through the skylights. "With you?"

An uncertain expression carved into his handsome features, but almost immediately transformed into his usual easy smile. "My boss thinks I've fallen head over heels. A man that desperate in love would want his woman near him 24/7." He leaned forward, lowering his voice to keep the conversation between them. "And if we're going to convince your family and my colleagues that we're in love, we need time to get to know each other's details and quirks."

"Details and quirks?"

He smiled and nodded at the coffee. "Like the fact that you don't drink coffee."

"Oh, right." She chewed on the end of her straw. Moving in with Nick would give her the opportunity to finish the renovations she'd started last year after purchasing her nineteenth century Gramercy Park home for her and her miserable ex. Might be good to get out of the place, renovate, start over. "What about…dating?"

"Dating?"

"Maybe I'm old-fashioned, but if I'm going to be living with you as your fiancée," she paused and glanced around the room, "I don't think we should see other people."

"Fair enough." He drew a sleek pen from the inside pocket of his suit coat, pulled a napkin from the dispenser, and scribbled out the terms. "Six weeks. Live together. No dating." He set the pen next to the napkin. "What else?" He took another sip of his coffee.

Marianne drew in a steadying breath, lowered her voice and asked what seemed like the obvious question, "Well…if you expect us to live together…um…what about sex?"

"Sex?" he choked out.

She closed her eyes and tried to ignore the shock stamped across his face. Three nights ago she'd popped out of a cake wearing silver spangles and this morning she was talking sex inside a Jamba Juice. *What was happening to her?*

"Yes, sex," she whispered.

And now she'd gone and said it again. Whispered, but still.

Nick dropped his voice, too, but the smile creasing his face was all kinds of wicked. And that voice. Even better lower. "Well, Marianne, anytime you want to add sex to our six-week agenda, let me know."

She swallowed hard and ignored the flutter in her stomach. "I'm fairly certain I can resist you for the six week duration of our engagement." His smile widened as if to say, "Don't count on it, sweetheart." "But that is not what I meant when I said no sex. I was *actually* referring to the rule that during our engagement there can be no sex outside the faux relationship."

"No sex even outside the relationship?" His eyes widened comically. "At all?"

Of course, she should have expected this type of

reaction from a man who went through women faster than his morning breakfast cereal, but it was still frustrating. Did he really think she'd meant sex between the two of them?

"No. Sex." From one of the four chambers of her heart, a determined voice whispered, *You can do this…stand your ground.* "We'd be living together, and I'd be your fiancée, so it's a matter of respect." Keeping her voice quiet, she rushed ahead. "And while 84 percent of all couples engage in premarital sex, obviously there will be no sex inside *this* relationship." She gave a short nod. "Six weeks, no sex."

"84 percent, huh?" He sipped his coffee. "I'd have guessed 95 percent," he said, scribbling a few words on the napkin. "No sex outside—or *inside*—the relationship." The way he said the words *inside the relationship* sent her brain into overdrive. "So—it's a deal?" he asked, as if it was the simplest contract this side of Manhattan.

She bit her lip, hard, not sure it was so simple. The probability of failure was high. A six-week engagement to a man who made her heart want to fly out of her chest and dive into his jacket pocket. A man who wouldn't know commitment if commitment bit him on his backside…oh, hells bells…on his ass. His tight, firm, sexy, *sexy* ass.

If she was going to commit to this plan, she needed to lock down her side of the bargain. "I'll give you six weeks and be the perfect fiancée as far as your colleagues are concerned, as long as you give me one weekend with my family and convince them we're madly in love."

"Madly in love?" Nick tapped his fingers on the table. "Only one weekend, right?"

"Oh, for heaven's sake."

"I'm in. Madly in love for the weekend." A teasing smile

formed on his face, more evidence that he was trouble. "Do we have a deal?"

Not allowing for second thoughts, Marianne thrust out her hand, all up-front and businesslike in her Zumba gear. If he was looking for an unemotional entanglement, she'd give it to him. And she'd get the perfect date in the process. "We have a deal."

He reached out to envelop her hand in his warm, masculine grip, and a zing of pleasure shot through her body like a bolt of lightning streaking across a summer sky. Her hand tucked in his, Marianne wondered what she'd just agreed to with this engagement. Six weeks of heaven? Or six weeks of hell?

Nick let go of her hand and slipped the napkin into the inside pocket of his jacket. "I'll draw up something more formal back at the office." All business as usual.

"No need. I trust you to be a man of your word."

He offered a short nod. "I'll messenger a key over to Smart Cupid, but if you want to settle in before it arrives, let the doorman know you're my fiancée, and he'll make sure you get into the condo safely."

"I'll wait for the key." Marianne was pretty sure if she told the doorman she was engaged to Nick Wright the poor man might have a shock-induced coronary and keel over.

He held her gaze for a long moment, one corner of his mouth lifted with undeniable mischievous intent. Almost as if she was…what? A *challenge*.

Still time to back out, a quiet, unadventurous voice whispered. Marianne took a moment to consider the well-timed warning. Men like Nick were trouble, and not just for a woman like her, for all womankind. Keeping him off the market for six weeks was like a public service, a Venus vs. Mars takedown allowing the female side a break from the risks involved in hooking up with a commitment-phobe whose skills of sexual persuasion rated high enough to fall off the charts. At least, she imagined his skills rated so high. Not that she planned to find out.

Then again, a little fact-finding mission might be fun, her inner siren whispered. Her stomach flipped.

She drew in a long breath and fought to stay calm. No need to get flustered and back out. This engagement was all business. He needed a short-term fiancée and she needed a date, preferably one that was guaranteed and as ridiculously sexy as Nick Wright. As long as she didn't tumble head over heels for the man, which she would not, the deal was a win for both of them. *Easy peasy, right?*

Nick shot her one of his killer smiles, and the butterflies in her stomach responded with a take-no-prisoners party.

Right.

Easy peasy, lemon squeezy.

Chapter Four

*I used to get the feeling, and sometimes I still get it, that I was
fooling somebody—I don't know who—maybe myself.*
—Marilyn Monroe

An hour later, after attempting to soothe her frayed
nerves with a class of restorative yoga, Marianne stood
on the corner of 23rd and Lex, sipped her anti-anxiety tea,
and gaped at the text on her phone. *Am I a genius, or what?*

A genius? She stared at the words. Took a breath. And
kept walking west toward her townhouse on the edge
of Gramercy Park. A list of appropriate responses raced
through her brain. *What were you thinking mixing me up
with your brother? Ambushing me outside the gym?* Or the
ever-pertinent, *I was wearing my Zumba gear, for crying out
loud.*

But instead of typing any of them, she stared at the
screen. Her six week engagement was an unholy bargain.

But six weeks was just one month, plus fourteen days, and what percentage of her soul could she lose in one month— and fourteen days? She scrolled to the next text. *Don't overthink his proposal, just say yes.*

Okay, fine, she'd said yes—but now she was definitely overthinking it. She quickened her pace. Had she really agreed to play house with the scorching hot financial attorney who'd been starring in her dreams for the past seven months, or was that just some crazy, Zumba-driven hallucination?

Not that they'd ever get married. Engaged, yes. A *fake* engagement, she reminded herself, twisting her key into the lock of the wraparound gate. Opening the entrance to the private park, she slipped through the wrought iron and scrolled to the next text. *Think of it as a six week test of your new sexy skills.*

Her new sexy skills. The words rolled around her thoughts. Sure, she'd popped out of a cake, but she'd also suffered a meltdown afterward and run off like some frazzled version of Cinderella— Did she really have any skills? Let's face it, this engagement deal was definitely a risk. If Nick found out she'd been the woman in the cake and felt disappointed, or worse, chuckled at New Girl trying sexy on for size, she'd *never* survive. Being jilted for a high-priced dominatrix was humiliating enough. Yes, that's correct. An *actual* dominatrix. Honestly, it wasn't the other woman's profession or her penchant for whips and chains, the betrayal and heartache would've been there no matter who he'd left her for. It was more the realization that the bondage mistress was her polar opposite. Like her ex-fiancé had never really known her.

Like she wasn't enough.

A stinging pain shot through her at the memory of how he'd declared her less-than-seductive in bed. *Timid. Ice queen.* Marianne had spent months wondering if he was right.

But not anymore.

She wanted to shed her buttoned-up image, embrace her sultry side, and experience the joys of being a woman.

Emotionally. Spiritually. *Physically.*

And Nick Wright was the perfect man to show her the ropes…not just the ropes, but maybe even one or two kinks in those ropes. So to speak.

Maybe she wasn't skilled in the sexual arts, but Nick was sexy personified. Even thinking about the easy, masculine way he'd cruised into Smart Cupid last week, dressed to the nines in his navy pinstripe suit, made her heart skip like a game of hopscotch. She'd been playing it safe, and cool, and by somebody else's rules for far too long. And for no good reason. The time had come to embrace her true self.

Her sexier self.

And if her ex showed up at the party with the dominatrix—she'd be prepared. Hopefully. Possibly. If she could work up the courage to commit to six weeks of close proximity—no—six weeks of an *engagement* to Nick Wright.

She took a long sip of her passionflower tea, needing more of nature's answer to Xanax to deal with her swirling thoughts, not to mention the string of texts from Jane, texts she'd been ignoring in favor of her new mantra, *Keep Calm and Marry On.* Even if she didn't feel calm, even if there would be no marriage. She read the rest of the messages in succession.

So, did you say, yes?

Or are you mad? Please don't be mad.

He needed a fiancée...you needed a date. Two plus two equals...

Personally, I think you should go for it! I mean, if you want to.

Just don't give me too many details. LOL.

After all, he is my brother.

So be good. But not too good. :)

Marianne let go a sigh. Even texting her friend was exhausting. She turned down her tree-lined street and typed out a message. *Not mad.* Not anymore anyway. Not entirely. *And I'm always good.* Truth be told, she'd spent her life meeting, or rather, exceeding expectations. She bit down on her bottom lip and typed out the question boomeranging around inside her brain before she could change her mind. Eyes closed, she pressed send. *But maybe I need to be bad?*

A response pinged back almost immediately. *Being bad sounds good.* Then another. *Maybe it's time to act on that mad crush of yours.*

A blush crept across her cheeks as she typed in her response. *How long have you known?*

The answer came back immediately. *How long have you*

been working here?

Marianne climbed the front steps of her brownstone, typing as she ran through a mental list of what she'd need to pack. *Six months.*

And when did you first get a look at my brother? Her stomach did a stop, drop, and roll at the memory. *Five months, fifteen days and six or seven hours ago.* She wrinkled her nose at the digital confessional. *Give or take.*

Ping.

That's how long I've known. <3

Nick rounded the corner of Mercer, heading home early—something he never did—to help his fiancée move into his place, a place that would be her home for the next six weeks. Sweet Jesus, talk about terrifying. He reached up to loosen the red power tie that suddenly felt too tight. *Six weeks, six survivable weeks.*

A new message buzzed into his phone, and he winced at the thought of another *Congratulations, welcome to the club* text. Or worse, another *Are we still on for Saturday night* invitation?

So much for no sleepovers, no back-to-back dates. His dating rules were about to take a serious beating. Thank God it wasn't football season. He pulled up the text. *Yankees game at the bar tonight. Up for it? Or are you spending the night with your fiancée?*

Not a congratulations. Not an invitation. Just the inevitable taunt from the guy who'd slipped a ring on his sister's finger a couple of months ago. And he would've fucked up the whole deal, too, if Nick hadn't been around. What was he doing giving Nick a hard time? He typed out a message in response to Charlie's text. *You're an asshole.*

A grin creased his face as he pocketed the phone. Always best to keep it short and sweet.

But no matter how much shit he took from his friend, he'd be spending tonight, and several more nights, with Marianne, learning as much about her as possible. If they were going to pull this off, he needed to know more than just her preference for tea over coffee. They needed to get intimate. Or know a few intimate details, anyway.

The sunshine reflecting off the casement windows of his pre-war building welcomed him home, but as he neared the entry, his gaze drifted to the sight of a pair of killer legs. He stopped in the middle of the cobblestone sidewalk and stared at the woman parked in the loading zone in front of his building, the one reaching into the backseat of an aquamarine Prius, the one with the legs. *Damn, his temporary fiancée got some back.*

Hell, she'd looked so sexy this morning in her skintight workout gear he'd gone momentarily off the rails and flirted with her. *His sister's off-limits friend.* He'd figured it was a one-time attraction. But now she was standing there on the sidewalk, all covered up in the knee-length skirt, and she still looked cute. Damned cute. Or maybe it was simply that Nick knew what lay underneath the prim hemline—a set of curves designed to conjure up some decidedly un-cute thoughts. Not that he should be noticing.

Despite her bodacious backside, Marianne McBride was not his type. Too uptight and inflexible. She drove a freaking

Prius, for Christ's sake. An *aquamarine* Prius. He shook his head. Probably a member of the Sierra Club, too.

Still, there was something about her…

But hooking up with a friend for a night of casual, no strings attached sex was not her style. Maybe he didn't know her well, but that much he knew. Marianne was nice. Probably liked nice guys, too, guys willing to settle down in some solar-powered, all-brick colonial in the suburbs, willing to drive matching hybrids and have enough mediocre sex to produce two appropriate kids.

No. Thank. You.

Still, watching her heart-shaped ass move in that little pencil skirt had him thinking of other slightly less predictable futures. A future of hot sex. Of teaching the good girl the thrill of being bad. Highly improbable futures. Good thing she was strictly off-limits because an all-brick colonial was not for him. No, he was committed to a totally hands-off, sex-free six weeks. He shook off his thoughts and walked over to the car

"Hello, Nick." Two simple words, but somehow full of accusation.

He smiled over at her. "Marianne."

All shapely legs and loaded tone, she stood on the edge of the cobblestone, clutching a cardboard box, blinking like an owl behind those ubiquitous glasses. A glance at the box told him it was overstuffed to the point of bursting with books. The only books he owned were law books and the thrillers his sister gave him every Christmas. Not a book guy. He reached for the box, but she tightened her grip as if the damn thing contained the secrets of the universe. He peered over the top of the cardboard. Romance novels and a Kindle, probably full of 'em. *So Little Miss Cardigan had a romantic side.*

"Let me help you." He shot her a smile meant to charm and pried the box from her grip.

She gave him a wary look, turned to grab another box from the front seat, and swiveled to close the door with the rounded edge of her hip. Her prim skirt rode a little higher on her thighs, and Nick dragged in a breath. *Man, like being kicked in the solar plexus.* He shook off his reaction a second time. Funny how he'd never been taken in by her rockin' curves before today. Probably had something to do with the tied-back hairstyle and the stressed-out attitude.

"Are you coming?" she asked over her shoulder, her tone clipped as she marched toward the front door. Right on cue—all uptight and inflexible.

Nick hefted the moving box onto his shoulder and followed his brand-new fiancée into the marble lobby. *Six weeks, six survivable weeks.* This partnership better be worth it, he thought, striding behind her. At least her swaying hips in that librarian-style skirt were a side benefit.

Behind the desk, his doorman gave him a knowing smile. "I hear love caught up with ya, huh, Mr. Wright?" Max said, hustling over to hold the door open, "Congratulations," he offered with a nod toward Marianne. "She's a real cutie."

A real cutie. Even his doorman knew the librarian wasn't his type.

"Thanks, Max," he said, his voice full of affection for the man. "Keep an eye on her for me. Don't let her get into any trouble."

"You can count on me, sir."

Nick glanced over at her, standing by the elevator, all

buttoned-up in her cardigan, unlikely to indulge in any kind of trouble, certainly not the fun kind. From the corner of his eye, he saw Max behind the desk, still smiling, and a twinge of guilt twisted in Nick's chest. Why did he have to be such an asshole? If not for Marianne, he'd be a man without a fiancée, a man without a shot in hell of scoring his partnership. So what if she was a little prim? She looked back at him over the top of her glasses. Okay, a lot prim. He could spend the next six weeks appreciating her killer legs. From a businesslike distance.

The elevator's bronzed doors slid open with a ding that echoed through the lobby like the death knell of his single man status. Marianne stepped inside and, with her chin pressed against a wayward flap of the cardboard, turned to peer at him over the top of the moving box. Leaning forward slightly, she pressed the inside button with her elbow to hold the door for him.

Nick couldn't remember the last time a woman had held an elevator for him. Kinda sweet. He walked over to the elevator, stepped inside, and the doors rumbled closed behind him.

He gave her a short nod and pressed the button for the tenth floor. "If I neglected to say it earlier—thank you. For saving my ass."

A nervous smile. A quiet voice. "You're welcome."

The elevator ascended with a whirr, and a palpable silence settled between them. Nick caught a glimpse of her in his peripherals. She stood ramrod straight, her tense gaze focused on the glimmering bronze ceiling. Nick shifted his weight from one refined Barker Black cap toe to another. The elevator buzzed higher—L, 1, 2, 3—its hushed, confined space growing close as the clean, sweet lemony scent of her skin floated toward him, a faint reminder of some sexy moment he couldn't recall…a kiss, maybe…the provocative tang of citrus on a woman's lips…or her hair, her skin.

Damn, he couldn't quite remember.

He imagined pinning Miss Cardigan 101 into the corner, breathing in her fresh scent, kissing her up against the electronic grid, letting every floor light up as he unlooped each button on her sweater, hell-bent on discovering what an impossibly proper girl kept tucked away under her sensible cotton.

Ding.

Whoa, what was that? Nick shook his head in an attempt to lurch back to reality. The elevator doors opened on ten and Marianne slipped past him in a breeze that smelled like the kind of summer vacations he'd always imagined. Not the kind he'd shared with Jane and Jake. The girl gliding past him vacationed in the warm sun on some white sand beach. She didn't float empty soda cans down the East River and call it a getaway. She didn't wish for a family trip full of laughter and fun. She didn't shoot off bottle rockets all summer and dream of something better. No, this girl *was* better.

In a strange fog, Nick stepped out of the elevator as the doors began to close, catching up to her outside his condo. Without a word of acknowledgment, she swiped the electronic key he'd messengered over and opened the heavy door into a stack of cardboard boxes. The seductive pull of her breezy scent evaporated like summer rain hitting the overheated Brooklyn sidewalk. Across the threshold, the espresso-stained floors were littered with neatly labeled containers. Clearly, this trip wasn't her first.

"Planning to stay six weeks or sixty years?" he asked.

She gave him a half-guilty, half-apologetic smile. "Just the six weeks, but I'm renovating my place in Gramercy Park—is it okay?" Her blue eyes blinked at him.

Like he had a choice. "Works for me."

He deposited his box onto the stack and followed her through the labyrinth of cardboard boxes muscling their way into his man-style home with its floor-to-ceiling windows and built-in sound speakers. She detoured from the narrow hallway into the bathroom, set her box on the marble vanity, and emptied its contents. He felt like he'd been kicked in the nuts. His sleek black counter was being overrun with a stash of girly products.

Nick stared at the impromptu beauty counter. He wasn't compulsive about much and that neurotic line of Bed, Bath and Beyond scared the shit of out him.

Instinctively, he glanced toward his subway-tiled, walk-in shower and felt the color drain from his face. An aggressively floral set of shampoo and conditioner bottles filled the shelf. Worse, they were pink. Not even a normal pink, but a bright fuchsia that screamed, *a woman is infiltrating your sanctuary*. He drew in a breath. Right now, he didn't care about her killer legs or how incredibly fantastic she smelled, his handsomely tiled, black and white bathroom was being overtaken by the feminine touch.

Nick turned around, ready to discuss the situation, but she was already gone. *What the hell?* He glanced down the hall. She was like a ninja. He took a few steps toward the back of the condo...and that's when he heard the humming coming out of his bedroom. Worse, the humming of some decades-old love song.

He drew in a breath and counted to ten. He could manage. Nick Wright wasn't about to be chased out of his own place or lose a partnership he'd worked his ass off to get, all because of a little bit of feminine gear and some humming. He was a professional. A reasonable, capable professional. He could take the noise. After all, she was doing him a major solid. He'd be wise to remember that, he thought, walking toward the sound.

Just outside the door, an old memory hit him, snapping into focus like a faded photograph made suddenly clear. A warm summer night, his mom sitting on the front steps of the row house, humming while she waited for his father to stumble home from some late-night poker game, probably three sheets to the wind, a fact she'd successfully hidden from his siblings, but not from Nick.

A stab of familiar guilt hit him hard. He despised being like his father, even in the smallest way. Sure, he didn't drink or bet the mortgage on the ponies, but when it came to women…he played 'em the same way. Love 'em and leave 'em. He stepped into the doorway and leaned against the frame. The strategy had worked for him, too, kept all his relationships light and fun and distant.

Until now…

Now she was here, humming in his previously sacrosanct, good-times-only bedroom.

And—fuck. She *was* a real cutie.

Neurotic maybe, but cute. His gaze took in the three hard-case Louis Vuittons lined up against the back of the closet, all emptied, everything starched and ironed, neat as a pin. Yeah, the neuroses ran deep. "I hope you left some room in there for me," he said, his tone laced with more than a fifth of irony.

Marianne turned around, blushing. "I'm sorry, I probably brought more than the basics, but better to be prepared, although I was wondering…about the whole closet…or rather, the bedroom, or well, the…um, the bed issue…" She drew in a breath. "Is this the only…the only…"

"The only bed?" He nodded and shoved his hands deep into his pockets. "To be honest, I never have overnight guests. Company, yes. Overnight, no."

"Oh." She adjusted the glasses against the bridge of her nose. "Female company?"

A smile played at the corner of his lips. "Is there any other kind?"

Her gaze fell to the floor in a trademark move he was already starting to recognize. Devil damned if he understood why, but the impulse to needle her was irresistible. All buttoned-up and serious, she was just so different from the sleek, ambitious legal eagles lined up to fill his empty bed on Saturday night.

But he had no business teasing his sister's adorably serious, strictly off-limits friend. No business at all. He bent his head to catch her gaze. "I'll sleep on the pullout in the office—without company."

She chewed on her bottom lip. Another trademark.

"Make you a deal," Nick said, walking over to grab her keys off the nightstand. "I'll park your sensible hybrid, and you…finish unpacking."

"But I need a few more things."

A few more things? He drew in another long breath and did a recount to twenty. *How much stuff did one small woman need?*

"Not tonight," he said. "Tonight we've got work to do. The rest can wait until tomorrow."

She eyed the keys as if considering a quick grab, but he tucked them securely into the front pocket of his suit pants. A smile edged across his face. No way was she diving in there for a set of keys. Not Little Miss Cardigan.

"Dinner, one hour." He gave her a wink and strode out of the bedroom. "My place."

Chapter Five

"I am good. But not an angel."
—Marilyn Monroe

Marianne folded the hemline of her skirt until it looked like an accordion. Precisely one hour had passed since the dinner invitation, and now, freshly showered, totally nervous, and semi-unpacked, she sat on the edge of the king-sized bed. Nick Wright's king-sized bed.

The other night at Temptation, she'd worn a mask just to work up enough courage to give him a simple happy birthday kiss. Now she was sitting in his one and only bedroom, wondering what it would feel like to roll around with him beneath the soft down covers of his one and only king-sized bed. *How had this happened to her?*

Happened in the sense that she'd pulled on a slinky dress, climbed into his birthday cake, and agreed to be his fake fiancée. That kind of happened to her. She drew in a breath. Everything was okay. She could handle being here in his souped-up SoHo bachelor pad.

Here.

Alone.

With Nick.

And her secret.

Her nerves fired on all cylinders. Her inner siren wanted out. Badly, and right now, but she couldn't just grab Nick by the shirt collar. Is that what Marilyn would do?

No. Marilyn would smooth her skirt, give the bed with its inviting down comforter one final glance, and slip barefoot into the hallway, all breathtaking innocence and sensuality. Much more subtle than the shirt collar grab, Marianne thought, kicking off her shoes.

After all, he was making dinner. Hiding away in the bedroom would be rude. Besides, she was looking to step out from behind her books and glasses and kick it up a notch. Hopefully, she wouldn't retreat into her shell or have some kind of panic attack. His reputation as a roll-me-hard tonight, don't-call-tomorrow kind of guy was notorious. Nick wasn't just stepping out of her shell. Nick was setting her shell on fire. A quick novena and she stepped into the hallway.

Whatever he'd been whipping up in the kitchen smelled fantastic, tangy and sweet. Italian, maybe. Her favorite. Despite the nerves, she was hungry. As a regular at Gristedes' takeout counter, a home-cooked meal sounded like a dream, and the fact that this particular dinner came with a side dish of sexy made it all the more deliciously dreamy.

As she approached the living room, Marianne's breath caught in her throat. The oversized windows, high beamed ceilings, and textured white walls were designed to catch the reflection of the city's lights, and the effect was so romantic, it took her breath away. And scared her to her death. Forty-two nights in this place…with Nick.

Her gaze drifted to the coffee table. A bottle of wine. Softly burning candles. Ed Sheeran's *X* album playing on the Bose. Her inner siren started dancing the merengue. Even Marianne knew what *X* meant. Sex, plain and simple. The correlation between music and intimacy topped most measurable charts, and documented research confirmed a well-curated playlist significantly increased the probability of sex. But there was the no-sex rule, the one her siren wanted to smash to bits, given that she'd not had sex in…well, in a very long time. Still, he couldn't be playing this music for her.

More likely, the music, the candles, the fake fire in the uber-contemporary fireplace, all of it was habit, typical womanizer moves, nothing to do with her. How could it be when she was the fade-into-the-background New Girl? A girl who normally objected to this kind of seduction-by-the-numbers on principle. But if she planned to use the next six weeks to break open her shell and embrace her sexuality, well, she needed to loosen up. The music helped.

And maybe the wine, too.

As she stood there, debating the merits of a Cabernet indulgence—a glass or two might facilitate the unmasking of the siren—Nick came out of the kitchen holding two plates piled high with food. Her mouth watered. A man who cooked was sexy. As if he needed any extra appeal.

He tossed his dangerous, full-wattage smile, the one that made her knees weak and her brain skid to a standstill. "Hope you like chicken parm."

Chicken parm. She glanced down at her feet—again,

speechless—her heart hammering against her ribcage. The music, the view…the man held her spellbound when she wanted to be adventurous and flirty. Yes, she loved chicken parm. *So tell him,* a voice inside her prodded, but no words came to mind. She blinked. *Blinking is not sexy. Respond. Verbally.* He'd made chicken parmesan—her all-time favorite. *Oh, please say something*, the siren urged, impatiently, *anything.*

"Love it." The two words tumbled from her lips in a voice a hint lower, huskier than usual, more Marilyn than Marianne. She raised her gaze to meet his. "I love it."

His audacious smile momentarily faltered as his eyes narrowed on her face with curiosity. *Dangerous, identity-busting curiosity.*

Panicked, she looked away and stabbed at her glasses. Marianne didn't want him to know she'd been the girl to jump out of his birthday cake. Or rather, in an alternative universe she'd secretly love him to guess, but in this reality— a reality where a man like Nick would never want the quietly resolved girl with the glasses—no. She simply needed a date and a chance to proceed with her plan to test drive her inner seductress, but with caution. *Be good. But not too good.* Nothing she couldn't handle, she thought, taking a seat on the rich leather sectional and praying for a miracle.

Nick set the plates down on the glossy black coffee table. "Then, let's dive in and get to work." He sat down next to her, close enough to make her heart rate jump up on the Fitbit scale. "Get to know each other's intimate details." He winked, flirtation his second nature.

She swallowed, hard. With him sitting so close, looking yummy and relaxed in his dark jeans and sexy bare feet, the probabilities were high that she'd have a tough time focusing on the details of her life. Details of any kind. Especially the intimate kind.

But Nick was right. If this plan was going to work for either of them, they needed to get down to the nitty-gritty. She took a long sip of the Cabernet he'd poured, grateful for something to do with her hands other than run them over his tempting, broad shoulders. Not much of a drinker, she'd feel the alcohol ease her nerves sooner than most. A good thing, too, because watching Nick dive into his dinner, all informal and at ease, made her feel cozy and at home. An unnerving feeling since her home was across town. Six weeks was all she'd get in this place.

Nick smiled over at her. "What do you say we play a version of twenty questions? Make the whole getting to know each other easier." He took a bite of the chicken and chewed. Wow, even the way he chewed was sexy. "If we're going to pull this off, we need to be on the same page with the details. I'll start, and we'll alternate questions until we've got it down."

Okay, counselor, she thought, ignoring her food in favor of another sip of the wine. She reminded herself he only wanted the partnership. Given detailed insight into her life, his ability to pretend he was in love with her could be dangerous to her infatuated heart.

"Obviously, I fell in love with you at first sight." *More wine, more wine, more wine.* "But where did we meet?"

"At Smart Cupid," she said, immediately. "Makes sense. Better yet, it's true."

"Not a very romantic meeting, though," he said, pointing his fork in her direction.

Not for him, maybe, but she could still remember feeling dizzy at the sight of him, so mind-blowingly handsome, the thought of him had wreaked havoc with her concentration for weeks.

"What if we met at a Yankees game?" he continued, and she blinked her way back to the conversation. "We both went for the same foul ball, your glasses went flying. I caught the ball and gave it to you and the rest, as they say, is…forever."

Her brows snapped together. "Except the statistical likelihood of a ball being hit toward you and you actually catching it is somewhere around .0008 percent." Another sip and she traded the wine for dinner. "Besides, I don't think anyone would believe I was at a Yankees game."

"Probably not."

"Not when the Mets are so much better." She took a bite of the chicken and sighed with pleasure. "This is delicious."

"Thanks." His eyes narrowed on her face. "Are you really a Mets fan?"

Another bite. "Really a Mets fan."

He shook his head and refocused on his meal. "Well, I won't be taking you to a game in the next six weeks," he said, as arrogant as any Yankees fan she'd ever known. "And you're right—better go with the truth. No one will believe I fell head over heels for a Mets fan."

Head over heels. Honestly, who'd believe a man as flat-out gorgeous as Nick would fall in love with her on any given day, much less head over heels?

"You're up, Mets fan."

With the easy comfort she so envied, Nick twisted some spaghetti onto his fork and lifted it to his kissable mouth. She wanted to be that comfortable in her own skin. She wanted another chance to kiss that mouth. Her fork clattered onto her plate. She felt a flush burn across her skin as she picked up the utensil and deliberately forked another piece of her dinner. No, her fingers hadn't just gone limp. No, she hadn't been staring longingly at his lips.

"Best childhood memory." Her words rushed ahead to cover her tracks.

Nick cocked an eyebrow. "That's a tough one...not many to choose from," he said, in a way that managed to seem boyish and vulnerable, as if the memories bothered him more than he'd let on. "You know about my father from Jane, the gambling, his taking off, leaving us with more debt than my mom could handle. A helluva mess. She worked a lot, my mom."

The glow from the television illuminated sadness in his impossibly blue eyes. A kind of loneliness, a feeling she understood completely. What she managed with statistics and computer code, he controlled with distance and swagger. But they each spent a lot of time alone.

"Occasionally, my father still contacts me."

"Really? I didn't think..."

"Jane doesn't know. Neither does Jake." He swirled more pasta onto his fork. "Mostly he calls when he needs a little money, sometimes just to remind me how much I'm like him." He raised his eyebrows. "But there were good times. Mostly, I remember Jane and Jake and me, and of course, Charlie, getting into trouble. Boosting lawn chairs, tossing eggs at windows and taking off, running like hell, trying not to get busted."

Marianne smiled at him over the rim of her glass. "Sounds like fun. Ever get caught?"

"Fun, yes. But did I get snagged?" He shot her a look that was all kinds of doubtful. "What about you? Ever get in trouble when you were growing up in…?"

"Manhattan," she said, finishing the question. "And, no, I was a rules girl. Never any trouble, always meeting expectations. But summers at the beach were fun. My cousins would come down to the house…"

"In the Hamptons?" Her short nod served as her response, so he continued, "I bet you were cute, all towheaded and tennis-tanned."

Such a heartbreaker, the man would flirt with a scarecrow if it wore lipstick and a skirt, but the truth was she'd never been all that cute. Too curvy, too young, she'd buttoned up around eleven years old and kept her sunburned nose in a book or computer, preferring the solitude to the teasing of the boys on the beach. Inexplicable curves, glasses, braces—the effect was awkward rather than adorable. "No, never very cute. Or towheaded. I spent a lot of time reading or banging on the PC."

Nick set his plate back on the coffee table and settled into the corner of the sectional. "That's right, you're my sister's computer girl, the one who designed the app she bet on last year. Nice job, by the way, backing Jane into a corner over Charlie."

"Well, she caused most of that trouble by herself, but…" She offered a small smile at his backhanded compliment, unsurprised to hear he was only putting the pieces together now. As far as he'd been concerned, she may as well have been invisible. "Before Jane gave me a job, I was hacking out a future as a mid-level broker."

"On Wall Street?" he confirmed. "Pretty ambitious stuff.

Why'd you leave?"

Anxiety twisted in her chest. No one had asked her that particular question in months, and it was a question too complicated to answer over chicken parm. She needed to tell him before her dad's homecoming—and she would—just not tonight. Her father's conviction and the resulting rumors had made her life as a trader too difficult to continue. But that was all over now—in the past where it belonged.

She offered a less complicated answer, one that was partly true considering how her engagement had unraveled after the arrest. "Man trouble?"

"Not of your own making?" *Touché on the reminder she'd called him out for his own brand of relationship trouble.*

She smiled. "No, not of my own making."

Nick returned her smile. "This was your last relationship?"

"My only relationship," she confessed. Well, only intimate relationship anyway, one that made her regret how long she stayed all reserved and buttoned-up. "And you? How many relationships are included in your romantic past?"

"Another good one," he said, furrowing his brow. "I don't know the number, not exactly, anyway." He eased back against the cushions, apparently nonplussed by the fact that counting his ex-lovers required an abacus and a formula-ready calculator.

Marianne shook her head, disinclined to talk about the letdown of her engagement, or Nick's serial dating ways, not now, not in this perfectly beautiful place, with this gorgeous guy. She'd wanted to release her siren a little bit, not discuss her cheating ex with her current sexy crush. Talk about dating mistake number one.

Maybe her ex-fiancé was right to call her hopeless, too

timid to be any fun in or out of the sack. Her heart flinched at the memory of her willing, tentative body, naked save a new pair of satin panties she'd picked up to surprise him, curling away, hiding from the look in his eyes as he spoke the words that tore her apart. *Timid. Hopeless. The original ice queen.* But she'd never felt frigid or cold. Awkward, yes. Unsure, absolutely, but never frozen inside.

No longer hungry, Marianne set her fork neatly on the plate and placed it on the table. "We should cover some of our favorites," she said, desperate to return to the former easy fun of the game. "Favorite color. Movie. Food?"

Nick waited, his intelligent gaze seeming to gauge her mood before deciding to take the left turn along with her. He smiled and said, "Blue, anything starring Steve McQueen, and The Dirty Burger from The Red Cat in Brooklyn." He shot her a *back to you* expression.

"Blue, *From Here to Eternity*, second only to *The Misfits*, and anything from the whole foods counter at Gristedes," she joked. "You are a good cook, but I buy takeout."

He picked up his glass and took a sip of the wine. "I like takeout. But I can teach you a few tricks in the kitchen—if you want."

She imagined heating things up in the kitchen, learning a trick or two, even moving past her man trouble. Maybe. Next question. "Favorite place in New York?"

Nick gave her another assessing look, and then, in one enviably smooth move, he took her hand and pulled her off the couch. "Come with me." He stepped around the coffee table and strode toward a room in the front near the windows.

"Where are we going?" she asked, stumbling in an effort

to equal his initial long strides.

"To my favorite place in New York." He slowed his pace and walked with her across the room and into his office. Once inside, he set his glass down on the desk, let go of her hand, and opened the closet to reveal a spiral staircase. "Up we go."

Her eyes narrowed at the precarious-looking steps to nowhere. "Really?"

"Really," he said, ushering her into the closet.

Marianne gave him an uncertain look, but he stood there, hands on his hips, looking like he wasn't going to take no for an answer. "Go ahead," he said, "I promise you won't regret it."

Her hands gripped the railing, and she started up the staircase. The metal felt cool on her bare feet, and as she climbed, her hips angled to negotiate the tight space. She glanced over her shoulder as she moved higher, and yes, he was looking.

A wicked smile creased his face, a clear sign he was enjoying the view. He ascended a few steps and leaned closer in order to reach past her and enter the lock's code. His nearness made her head spin, and she held the railing a little tighter. His smile widened. "Keep going."

She pressed open the door and was rewarded with a view of the city that left her completely breathless. "No wonder this is your favorite place in town."

"Reason I bought into the co-op."

"Do you—?" Her sweeping gesture encompassed the rooftop garden.

"No, I hire someone to take care of the place."

Her eyes took in the border of wild lavender and

overflowing pots of green leaves and bright red flowers, a small natural oasis suspended against the urban skyline. "Oh, I'd love to take care of this place—it's beautiful."

"You should plant something while you're here. Add your touch." But all she heard were the words, *while you're here*, a clear reminder of the fact that she was temporary.

He placed his hand on the small of her back. "If you stand in this corner, you can see all the way to Brooklyn."

His hand moved away, and he hooked both thumbs through the belt loops of his jeans. So relaxed and laid-back. She wanted to feel that way, wanted to crawl inside that kind of comfort. She turned back toward the view. The white noise of the city filled the silence between them. Standing with Nick, looking out over the city, she felt light years from her usual routine, and couldn't remember the last time she'd felt so charmed by something unexpected.

"A world away," she said.

"A world away," he agreed, a distant expression carved into his handsome face. "A far cry from Brooklyn." The sardonic timbre in his voice was not lost on Marianne, and she considered asking for more details, but the easy cool she admired was already back in his voice. "Of course, this is where I proposed."

The shift in his manner was so lightning-quick that she blinked, not quite following.

But when he grinned over at her, the pieces fell back into place. "Got down on one knee, the stars shining above us, the city at our feet, a hot kiss at the end."

Her cheeks warmed and she wondered what that dreamy moment would feel like with a man like Nick. "Quite a romantic proposal."

"Quite." He looked over at her, smiling that irresistible smile, and there was no reason to wonder why women fell at his feet. His gorgeously naked feet, she thought, glancing down at the flagstone. He playfully bumped her shoulder with his, more Brooklyn kid than SoHo bad boy. "If you were to be kissed in this place…how would you want to be kissed?"

"To be kissed?" She bit down on her bottom lip. He was talking about kissing. Not that his casual mention of kissing her, here, in this beautiful place meant anything. Flirtation was a simple reflex for the man. Nothing to do with her.

He bent his head to try and catch her eye. "A kiss may be required at some point."

"Required?" Marianne drew in a steadying breath, but it failed to calm her nerves. He smelled so good, so clean and masculine, but she wasn't 100 percent sure about the whole siren, unkinking the ropes situation. If he was going to flirt with her, the way he was flirting now, she needed all her faculties to manage the hypnotic effect.

He leaned closer, a teasing expression on his face. "Most engaged couples do kiss."

Of course, he was right. Statistically speaking. If she and Nick were going to make their faux engagement look real enough to convince his colleagues and make her ex wish he'd never shacked up with leather and lace, then…kissing was called for. Besides, kissing wasn't sex. Kissing was kissing. Kissing she could handle.

A quick one. Semi quick, anyway.

Like the night of his birthday party. Except without the Cinderella finale.

Ready or not. She adjusted her glasses against the bridge

of her nose. "Did you know on average, a person spends two weeks of his or her life kissing?" *Obviously, she'd not been ready.* She was making the whole thing sound like a science experiment. "Or more precisely, 20,160 minutes." She blinked twice. *Wow, had she really just reduced kissing to a calculation?* Talk about un-sexy.

"Interesting stat."

Her heart started racing. The closer he came, the more her nerves fired in a strange, new, haphazard way that confounded her thoughts. She forced her brain to focus. "Yes, and did you know that a real kiss quickens your pulse to over one hundred beats a minute?"

"No, I did not." Looping a wayward strand of her hair around his index finger, he tilted forward until he was close enough to whisper. "But I think it's a theory worth testing."

He smiled. She smiled back. His hands moved to frame her face, tilting the roof on an invisible axis and seemingly tossing them into the middle of the city's twinkling lights and the stars. And then...he kissed her. Her eyes dropped closed as his lips moved across hers in a sweet, mesmerizing kiss that seemed to shift the ground beneath her feet. A sigh fell from her parted lips, inviting him closer. And he kissed her. Kissed her the way he'd kissed her in her dreams and, when he pulled away, the lingering effect left her dizzy.

They stood there for a moment, his fingertips against her flushed cheeks, her breath shallow and soft, both seemingly surprised by the electricity between them.

Another glimmer of curiosity surfaced at the back of those deep blue eyes, and Marianne felt her stomach flutter. If she kept kissing him, he'd figure her for the girl in the cake before midnight. Would he call off the deal? Or worse, be embarrassed for her? The New Girl who jumped out of his birthday cake and ran. She pressed her palms against her belly. The thought of Nick feeling sorry for her was unbearable. Not when all she wanted to do was keep kissing him.

He took a step back, and a small smile broke out across his face, transforming him immediately from sexy-sexy to sexy-adorable. *So much harder to resist.* "Best guess—think your heart made it to one hundred beats?"

She looked up at him as if coming out of a daze. One hundred? Try one thousand. Any faster and her heart would explode like one of the stars winking down from the darkening sky.

He reached out and pulled the heavy frames away from her face. "Maybe we should try one more?"

If she wanted to embrace her feminine mystique and declare her sexuality fully emancipated, or at least emancipated enough to hold her own with her ex's new lover, now was the time to go for it. Forget resistance. *Go for an uninhibited stunner of a kiss.*

"I think I could pencil one in," she said, sounding more like an academic than a siren.

Still smiling, he bent his head to kiss her a second time, but as he drew close, a tsunami of panic overtook her and she backed away, suddenly afraid of letting go, of being truly seen. She'd hidden for so long behind her cardigans and books, always safe and out of harm's way, never really noticed or admired. She'd always been happy enough that way, content to tap away on her keyboard or read a novel. Another kiss might illuminate the truth that she was the runaway cake jumper, and despite her recent attempts to break out of her shell, Marianne avoided the spotlight. She wasn't ready for the truth. Not tonight. *Maybe not ever.*

She bit down hard on her bottom lip. If she was honest, some small part of her hoped he'd recognize her; wanted him to see her as more than the nerdy new girl with the glasses — *see* her, the *essential* her — but that was an impossible fantasy. Hiding was safer. She eased her glasses from his grip and settled them back on her nose, all traces of her inner siren a distant memory. "Next week. I'll pencil it in next week."

"I'll take the rain check," he said, as easy as basic math.

And then Nick Wright did something unexpected. A loose curl had fallen from her usual, pinned back style, and he reached out to brush it away from the curve of her cheek with his thumb. So gentle. So endearing.

So charming that Marianne's heart fell, just a little bit more, temporarily in crush with the unattainable man who was all wrong for her. Trouble was, what was she going to do about it?

Chapter Six

"The list of things women like is long and contradictory."
—mantelligence.com

L *ast night was a close call.*
Nick slammed shut the leather cover of his tablet computer, wondering why the hell he'd kissed her on the rooftop. Chalk it up to habit—see an attractive woman, swoop in for the kiss. But she was off-limits. The deal was simple, six weeks of a platonic engagement in exchange for the partnership he'd always dreamed about. And then there was his sister's warning and his own determination to keep things hands-off.

The whole damned situation was playing tricks with his head. Marianne was pretty in an awkward, utensil-dropping way—and there was something else, too, something he couldn't name, something familiar, that made him weigh the pros and cons of kissing her again. But if he were smart, he'd steer clear. He enjoyed being the guy with a new woman every other week. No commitment, no one to hurt.

Besides, his fiancée was not his type. He'd been right to peg her as buttoned-up and uptight, even if she could be warm and intelligent, too. He tapped his fingers on top of the tablet. Yeah, something about her didn't add up. And he liked things to add up.

He liked straightforward answers based on fact, not suppositions and intuition, and he made sure every case that crossed his desk reached a clean resolution, albeit generally in his favor. He put in long hours at the office and dug deep into case law to get the job done. His workaholic ways and lack of interest in commitment left little time for mysteries or love—Nick was fine with that. Keep it forthright. Keep it light. He didn't like puzzles. A challenge, yes. A conundrum, no.

But he liked Marianne.

He liked her bright blue eyes. Liked her citrusy scent and the impossibly familiar definition of her killer legs. Liked her unexpected vulnerability. And he liked the idea of seeping under her reserve and causing a total meltdown. Loved the idea, actually.

Oddly enough, his gut told him she'd like that, too. But none of it made sense. Why had he never noticed her before? Certainly it wasn't all about the Zumba gear. No, she didn't add up. Blushing one second, negotiating the next. He'd figure it out. His fingers tapped a deliberate rhythm on his desk, trying to unravel the puzzle that was Marianne McBride.

"You've got that lost-in-love look on your face there, partner."

Nick's gaze slid in the direction of the sarcastic remark and sure enough, Drew Evans was at the other end of it. Prick. "Not a partner yet," he said in an even, professional tone.

Jesus, that guy was always around to cause trouble. Like Nick, he was a senior associate. But unlike Nick, he was a slacker, all play, no ethics, and zero hours burning the midnight oil. Destroying a colleague to get ahead was closer to his modus operandi. More than likely, he'd started the rumor that led Nick to need a fiancée. Son of a bitch was ruthless.

Evans sauntered into the office, uninvited. "Word around the firm is your confirmation's just a matter of time. Now that you're engaged and Jeffers is satisfied you're not banging his ex-wife. All so convenient and well-timed, if you ask me."

"Back off, Evans."

He offered a tight smile and tossed a research file on Nick's desk as if he were the man in charge. "Consider me backed off, Nick," he said, emphasizing his sarcasm with a set of air quotes. "But I can't wait to get a look at your fiancée tonight."

"Tonight?" he asked. Not like they socialized regularly. Or, ever.

"The partner event. Can't wait to see if you can pass off this new fiancée of yours as the real deal. If you've even got a woman lined up." He offered a casual shrug and turned to leave. "Either way, watching you go down in flames is going to be the highlight of my year."

Son of a bitch. Nick's jaw tightened. *The damned partner event.* He'd assumed the event would be partners and senior associates only—as usual. He'd forgotten they included spouses. Hell, he'd never even considered it, but now that he was engaged, the invite extended to Marianne. He bit back a curse. Tonight could fast-forward his professional life to its friggin' conclusion. Thank God they had some quality time together last night—they just might be able to pull this off. Either that, or his colleagues would take one look at Marianne's starched cardigan and know she was a fraud. Strike that—*he* was the fraud.

If Dan Morgan caught on, not only would he lose his shot at the partnership, he'd lose his job, his reputation, and the respect of the partners. Pretty much career suicide. He paced across the office. He needed a loophole. An escape clause. A get-out-of-the-partner-event-free card. Except there was no way of getting out of tonight, not since his engagement had become all the talk around the firm. Better to focus on getting the details right, making sure they had their act down well enough to fool everyone. Was there a detail he'd forgotten? All of a sudden, his tie felt like it was strangling him.

Something like…*a ring?*

Nick couldn't breathe. He needed a ring to seal the deal, make it look official. He forced the thought from his mind and pulled at the collar of his pristine white shirt.

A ring? Was he really going to give her a ring to complete the illusion? Jesus, he'd lost his mind. Was he supposed to stop into a diamond mart on the way home and pick up some Neil Lane knock-off? This wasn't an episode of *The Bachelor*, for Christ's sake. This was Real Life. He paced to the other side. Well, Real Life for their little Liars Club of Two.

Shit.

No ring. It was too much. Besides, even if he decided

to go with a ring, with the current state of his luck, his new fiancée would spend the night decrying the politics of blood diamonds, which would be worse than the damn cardigan. He scrubbed his face with his hands. A ring would definitely make his farce of an engagement seem real, and a real engagement was critical to winning the partnership. Nick couldn't risk anything going wrong tonight. Evans wasn't the only associate hoping he'd fail. Hell, there was probably an office pool.

"Plan on coming to the event tonight?" Standing in the doorway, his boss fired off the question, phrasing it in a way that was really a statement. Amazing. Like some kind of Jedi mind trick. Nick definitely needed to develop that skill.

Dan continued. "I want to introduce you to a few of the senior partners, start garnering some goodwill. Put the business with Jeffers's wife in the rearview."

Nick stood, grateful for his boss's support. "Absolutely."

"And bring your fiancée. I'm looking forward to meeting the woman who stole your heart, not to mention saved your ass," he joked in his deep baritone. "Bet she's impressive as hell."

He nodded his agreement. "Like a high-yield portfolio, sir."

Not exactly romantic, but better than nothing.

Maybe. A vague look of misgiving crossed Dan's face. *Maybe not.* His boss wasn't the top dog at one of Manhattan's leading firms for no reason. He knew bullshit when he smelled it.

If Nick planned to survive the situation, he needed to step up his game. "We'll see you tonight, sir."

"See you tonight," Dan agreed, turning to leave Nick

with his thoughts.

Not for the first time, Nick wondered what he'd been thinking when he'd come up with this plan. A six-week engagement to a woman who was practically a stranger? He tore both hands through his hair. Arrogant and reckless, just like his old man. This was why he played love cool. No entanglements. No issues.

Now he could potentially lose everything.

He whipped around, turning his back to the door, and landed a right hook into his open palm. His simple engagement deal was edging closer to a DEFCON One situation, and if he planned to satisfy some of the more traditional partners, not to mention his skeptics, Nick needed proof of love. He needed a ring and a proposal. He linked his fingers behind the back of his neck and stared up at the ceiling. How the hell was he going to manage that?

Marianne stared at the calculation on her computer screen. She'd run the numbers nineteen times and the result was still the same. But it couldn't be. The kiss she shared with him last night could not be statistically significant; it was just a close call, an experiment, baby steps on her journey toward sexual freedom. If it meant anything more, he would've recognized her.

She stabbed at the keys and reentered the data—the number of minutes she'd spend engaged to Nick—a figure totaling roughly 59,040—and its correlation to the likelihood that she'd kiss him again. Oh, hells bells, she already wanted to kiss him again.

Finished, she sat back in the office chair and pressed the keys to run the algorithm one more time...and...yes, the same result appeared on the screen. According to the love matrix she'd designed, she and Nick were a perfect match, which was, of course, totally impossible.

If they were a perfect match, he wouldn't haven't sounded so panicked when he'd called about his firm's event tonight. Okay, maybe it was her panic echoing through the line. Nick had sounded cool and casual, his usual Bond-like self. Shaken, not stirred. She drew in a breath. He might be chill, but her nerves were definitely shaken. Tonight would be their first real test, a chance to prove they were happily engaged, in love...

A perfect match. Well, technically there was no such thing as *perfect*, but anything in the 97th percentile or higher was as close to perfect as statistically possible. They scored a 98.7.

How could she live up to that? With a score that high, if she continued to test her sexy skills by kissing him, her feelings could catch fire, and with Nick sure to bolt after the six weeks—could she handle it? She'd already been hurt, and badly; another dose of pain might crush her. Her fingers flew across the inset keyboard, adjusting the chemistry aspect of the dating algorithm. There had to be a fix.

Yes, she needed a date, and if she was honest, another baby step toward emancipating her inner seductress sounded good, too. But why didn't he recognize her? He'd kissed her twice now, if there was more between them than a one-sided fascination, he ought to be able to see her. *Really see her.*

Typical. She wrinkled her nose at the screen. *Blind and arrogant.*

But sweet, too. *Dagnabbit.*

The tapping of a pair of high heels and the bitter aroma of coffee alerted Marianne to the fact that her boss was cruising over to her desk. Like most days now, Jane sported a smile on her face and a coffee carrier in her hand, but unlike most days, she had a hot pink cocktail dress flung over her shoulder.

"For your inner siren." Jane set down the carrier and presented the dress as if she were delivering the Holy Grail. "In case you happen to have a sexy date night—with your fiancé."

Marianne took one look at the strapless little number, swiveled away from her desk, plucked the dress from her friend's hand, and walked over to the closet. The one on the far side of the office. No way was she falling for the dress gambit a second time. She'd have to get through tonight in her best cardigan and skirt combination.

Jane followed. "Are you excited about tonight? Do you need anything? Shoes, maybe? A trip to the lingerie store?"

A trip to the lingerie store? Marianne whirled around to face her. "So you know about his big work event?"

"Nick might have texted me…"

She rested her hands on her hips. "And does he know about the cake jumping?"

Jane held up her hands in surrender. "Absolutely not. Not from me. Or Charlie."

Marianne spun around and marched straight back to the desk. She needed to put some distance between herself and the little pink dress calling to her from the closet. She was a serious person. Not a woman tempted by a dress or a field trip to buy underwear. "I can't believe he doesn't know…

doesn't recognize me."

A perceptive smile on her face, Jane lifted a grande herbal tea from the carrier and handed it to her. "Love is blind."

"Love?" Her brows snapped together in annoyance. "Who said anything about love?"

Jane parked her denim-clad behind on the edge of the desk. "Hate to break it to you, especially now that you're engaged, but despite his miserable track record, Nick is more than a one-night-only kind of guy. He's got more substance than he'll admit."

Marianne sipped at the tea. Images flashed through her mind like a Technicolor filmstrip. Nick's hands framing her face…his lips on hers…his thumb against her cheek.

Jane leaned over and peeked at the open database window. "Wondering just how hot a compatibility score can get?"

She flipped the tablet cover shut in one quick motion, her face flaming. The overheated matrix score she shared with Nick was a mistake. She was certain. The man couldn't count his past relationships on two hands…and two feet. Conversely, she'd only had one relationship, a total disaster of Titanic-sized proportions. On a groan, she sank down into the chair.

How could she convince her ex, not to mention her family, she'd moved from Jilted Lover to Hot Fiancée of a man like Nick? Yes, he absolutely turned her inside out, but despite what the matrix said, despite last night's kiss, when he looked at her, all he saw, all he could *possibly* see, was a woman in an unadventurous navy skirt and ivory cardigan. She set the tea down on the desk and yanked hard on the bottom of the sweater.

Her whole life she'd been nerdy and tentative with her thick glasses and quiet resolve. While her classmates had indulged in Seven Minutes in Heaven, she'd been hiding away with her books and writing computer code. Always the good girl. An image she'd allowed, or maybe, even one she'd created. A small pain stabbed at her heart.

Inside, she'd always been more than that quiet, cautious girl, so why had she never tossed the cardigans? Fear? A need to always do the right thing? Maybe. But what had chasing that standard gotten her? A pink slip and a scandalous ex-engagement written up on Page Six—thankfully they'd neglected to add a postscript, *Jilted for former dominatrix*. For these small miracles, she owed the tabloid gods a kiss. Or a gift basket.

But she hadn't rallied her nerves and climbed into that cake for nothing. To heck with page six. Maybe it was time to stop living up to expectations and simply start living.

She wrinkled her nose and glared at the closet. That darned dress was calling to her.

Jane tapped her fingers on top of the closed tablet. "Know what your inner siren needs?

"A lobotomy," she joked, thinking it was as good a place to start as any.

"No." Jane laughed and shot her a look of excited anticipation. "A makeover."

"A makeover?" Marianne sat up in her chair. Serious women—even ones reconsidering their inflexible standards—did not get makeovers. She shook her head, but her friend was prepared for objections.

"To make you feel more confident with the partners.

Nothing major, just a little TLC to remind you how beautiful you are—inside and out." Her friend flashed that persuasive smile and tugged on her ear. *Never a good sign.* "C'mon, M.A., you can trust me."

Marianne scrunched up her face, starting to fold, half interested in creating a brand-new image, half certain this was not a good idea. "Fine," she said. "But I'm keeping the glasses."

"Yes." Jane pumped her fists into the air, walked over, and pulled Marianne out of the chair. "We're keepin' the glasses."

"But what about the office?" she said, glancing back at her desk, double-timing her steps to keep up as her friend strode over to the closet.

Jane tossed out another big fat grin and grabbed the dress. "Good thing I'm the boss."

Chapter Seven

*"I don't know who invented high heels, but all women owe
him a lot."*
— Marilyn Monroe

As music drifted from the speakers, Marianne stood in
front of the floor-to-ceiling windows at the edge of the
living room and stared at her reflection. Outside the SoHo
lights twinkled, winking up at her as if in on her secret and,
as she gazed up at the stars, the darkening sky at her feet, she
felt transformed.

Dressed in the hot pink, strapless number from the
closet, her hair a shade lighter, equal parts blond and sandy
brown, she looked…well…still serious, still like herself, but
different. Equal parts siren and Marianne.

Jane's stylist had cut her shoulder-length mess into a
stylish bob that seemed to flatter every curve of her face. Incredible, really, what the man had accomplished with a pair

of scissors and massive quantities of tropical-smelling hair products.

Adjusting her glasses on the bridge of her nose, she twisted to glimpse the pièce de résistance, a pair of high-heeled, strappy gold and pink sandals that were absolutely to die for. Sure, she'd been testing out the occasional high heel in her quest to embrace her sexier side, and she'd worn the red stilettos, but these beauties were different. Delicate and sweet, but sexy, too. A perfect complement to the dress.

When she'd agreed to go tonight, she'd been terrified, completely certain she'd fail to impress. But Jane had said *trust me*, and her friend had come through in spades. Marianne looked sexier than she'd ever looked. More importantly, she *felt* sexier. Vivacious and free, even a little bit beautiful.

Turning from the window, she walked to the armchair and picked up the new cardigan she'd purchased at Saks. Soft ivory silk, with gold sequined paillettes, the sweater made every other sweater she owned envious. Not wanting to cave completely to the idea that a woman needed to be packaged or made over to be desirable, Marianne had insisted on the sweater, the way she'd insisted on the glasses.

But she had slipped into LensCrafters and upgraded her tortoiseshells to a sultry pair of golden cat-eyed frames adorned with a smattering of crystals at the temple, the perfect amount of bling. Never a believer in fairy tales, Marianne felt like some kind of modern day Cinderella.

No statistics. All magic.

Her phone rang. She glanced at the screen and picked up. "Jane?"

"Are you wearing the dress?"

Marianne smiled at her friend's less-than-traditional greeting. "Yes, and it's beautiful. But are you sure?" She bit down hard on her lower lip and glanced down at the dress. "Maybe it's too sexy for a work function."

"Trust me on this one." The smile in her voice came straight through the phone. "Just stick to the plan and you'll be the hottest fiancée in the place."

"Right." *Stick to the plan.*

Be sociable. Be sweet. Be charming.

Be careful.

Marianne wrapped her arms around her torso to control the shivers of excitement and anxiety coursing through her body at the thought of a real date with Nick. Jane had been right, a little TLC, and already she felt more confident. *The hottest fiancée in the place.* "Wish me luck."

"Are you wearing the strappy gold sandals?"

She glanced down at the sexy little numbers. "Yes."

"Then Marianne?"

"Yes?"

"You don't need luck."

• • •

The sapphire ring burned a hole in his pocket.

Nick was about to give a ring to his fake fiancée. His mother's ring, the one he kept in his office safe because he didn't have the balls to pawn it when she'd asked him to. Not like his mom would ever know. Marianne would wear it for a few weeks and then—boom—right to the pawnshop. No more sentimental bullshit.

Jesus, he was going to give a woman a ring. He shook his

head. If there was ever a time to book an appointment with a psychiatrist, it was now. Trying to pass off a blind date as the love of his life was crazy, more like a roll of the dice than a calculated risk. He kneaded the muscles at the back of his neck. Maybe he was more like his father than he wanted to admit.

But unlike his old man, Nick refused to run. If tonight ended in a flameout, he'd survive. The end of his partnership bid. Hell, the end of his career. Whatever came next, he'd face it, straight on. He'd survived worse. A quick swipe of his electronic key activated the lock, and he stepped inside the condo. But the place felt different.

The door shut behind him with a click. Music floated down the hall, and not just any music, sexy blues music.

He took a few steps toward the living room. An inviting, citrusy scent mixed with the burn of the vanilla candles Jane had given him last year. He liked it. Funny, he was so used to walking into a dark, empty apartment that he never gave much thought to what a less-empty one might feel like.

Marianne had brought warmth along with her overloaded Kindle and cool, starched skirts, and surprisingly, Nick was pleased with the change. Not that he was going to be changing his rules anytime soon. Relationships weren't for him.

He enjoyed his routine—long hours at work, dates that ended in great sex, an occasional beer at Temptation, dinner with Jane. He liked his habits, everything was easy and fun, and yes, he confessed, maybe a little shallow. He'd never allowed himself to consider it until now, but his patterns felt a bit hollow. His dating rules purposefully left little room for a woman in his life, but he had to admit that it was nice to come back to a place that felt like a home. Nick hadn't felt at home in a long, long time.

He stopped at the end of the hall, rested his shoulder against the wall—and whoa—he didn't need to be concerned about her starched cardigan exposing his engagement scam. He needed to worry about one of the partners suffering heart failure. Holy hell, when he called to tell her about tonight, she promised to be ready, but he'd been expecting a knee-length skirt, maybe an upgraded cardigan. Marianne had been talking about a whole different ballpark. *Holy shit.* Simply watching her from across the room made his mouth go dry.

Lost in the sultry rock song playing, her hips moved in a slow deliberate semicircle as if dancing a sensual rumba. Released from her usual pulled-back style, her golden brown hair swung in a soft sheet past her chin, and he felt a sudden urge to sift its weight through his fingers as if it were pure silk.

Nick hadn't even started on the dress. Man, that was one helluva dress. Enough to bring a room full of investment attorneys to the closing table. Not at all what he'd been expecting. The prim skirt and sweater combo had been replaced by a cocktail dress that was spectacular, but not nearly as spectacular as the curves swaying to the music, filling out the lines of the dress, coasting past full hips to a pair of strappy sandals. Nick bit back a groan. Those killer legs let loose in a pair of high heels practically knocked the wind out of him.

"Holy hell," he said, standing at the edge of the room.

Startled, she turned to look. Right. At. Him.

Damn.

Nick scrubbed his face with his hands. If the back of the

dress was spectacular, then the front was…*holy shit*.

She took a step toward him, stumbling a bit in those smokin' hot stilettos. "Hi, I hope you don't mind…"

Her words drifted past him, but none of them mattered. He was struck by the voice, all sweet and sultry. The voice… the curves…the stumble. How could he not have seen it before?

He felt the air rush from his lungs and the kick in his stomach. Only one other time in his life had he felt this hammer-to-the-gut type feeling. At his party, the moment the cake girl wished him happy birthday in that hushed, knock-me-out whisper. He stood there, leaning against the wall, his hands buried in his pockets.

Surprise, surprise.

Little Miss Cardigan was his cake girl. Un-fucking-be-lievable. All this time, she'd been right under his nose, stammering and blushing, hiding beneath her buttoned-up sweaters and horn-rims. She was like a naughty librarian fantasy transported into his living room, all glasses and pencil skirts. A crystal-clear image skyjacked his brain—his hands tracing the curves of those hips she concealed with wool skirts, skimming down her toned, upper thighs, caressing those killer legs. A crazy-wide grin broke across his face. "Hey."

"Hi," she said, tucking a strand of blond-streaked hair behind her ear in a gesture that was equal parts cute and seductive.

Same girl, all right. Same addictive, vulnerable-sexy way.

He kept smiling as a half dozen puzzle pieces clicked into place. His instantaneous reaction to her and the way she climbed into his thoughts. Jane's willingness to set him up with a fiancée. Charlie's inexplicable inability to find her.

But most especially, his protective feeling, his whole wrap-cake-girl-in-a-protective-jacket-and-take-her-home-with-me response suddenly made sense. On some level, he must have recognized her, known it was the New Girl, or rather, Marianne.

Nick couldn't believe his luck. The situation was *perfect*.

He had an ideal temporary fiancée, a partnership waiting to be confirmed, the chance to get cake girl out of his system. Ever since that night, he'd wondered why one innocent kiss had left him with a short-term obsession, but clearly, his fascination was about the mystery, not the actual woman. Now that the puzzle was solved, now that he knew who she was, well, odds were good he'd be back to living by his dating rules in under six weeks.

"Nick, are you okay? You look a little strange."

"I'm fine…" he said with a reassuring smile. "You look amazing."

In fact, she looked…perfect.

"Really?" She chewed on her bottom lip, one of the crazy-sweet, seductive gestures that made him want to kiss her until she was breathless. "Are you sure it isn't too sexy?"

He walked over to where she stood by the window. "Sexy enough to send one or two of the older partners into cardiac distress."

Her brows rose above the glittery new glasses. "Is that too sexy?"

Nick chuckled and took her hands in his. His fiancée was his cake girl, and while the New Girl had been off-limits, the woman standing in front of him was a different deal. He made a low sound of appreciation in the back of his throat. "Not in my book. You look absolutely perfect."

A small giggle of pleasure bubbled up from her throat. "Well, then, we better go before I lose my nerve." She turned away, but he pulled her back, tugging her against his chest. She blushed and smiled at him. Nick felt a strange light-headed rush. Damn, he did not want to go to casino night with the partnership. He wanted to play his own games right here at home.

In bed with his sexy new discovery.

And he wanted answers. He wanted to know how she'd ended up in his cake, why she'd kissed him and run, and if she'd be willing to break the no-sex rule for the remainder of their agreement. Because he sure as hell was willing.

But nothing else had changed—not for him. This was still a short-term arrangement. A *business* arrangement. He wanted to add a little extra spice to an already sweet deal. Nothing wrong with that. Yes, he was proposing, but to satisfy his colleagues, and with a temporary ring—a prop, really—more like a loaner ring than an engagement ring.

Still, there was no doubt that he wanted her like crazy, and if *all* his feelings fell into the temporary category, why were his hands sweating? *Don't even think about it.* He shoved aside the niggling doubt, reached into his pocket, and pulled out the battered leather box. Her eyes widened and stared at the small square between the two of them. Nick wasn't sure who was more shocked.

"Is that what I think it is?" Her quiet words tumbled out as his own raced ahead of his brain.

"It's a loaner," he said.

It's. A. Loaner.

If there was even a single molecule of romance in the moment, his words sucked them out of the room as if they were a fleet of those extra-powerful Dysons. His fingers closed around the square box in a vise grip. *God, did he have to sound like such an asshole?* Not that their engagement was romantic. This was a business deal with an agreed upon expiration date. But still, it's a loaner? *Shit.* He'd meant to reassure her. Or himself. Or…hell, he didn't know. He was holding a box with a ring in it, for Christ's sake. But he hadn't meant it to sound so calculated and defensive. So *temporary.*

"A loaner." She adjusted her pretty, new glasses in that nervous way of hers, her eyes locked on the small box extending into the space between them.

Nick cleared his throat. He needed to backtrack. "You don't have to wear it. I just thought if we're trying to convince everyone we're getting married," he said, choking on the last word, "an engagement ring might close the deal."

Marianne blinked over at him as if she could see straight through him. Like she saw all the reasons he kept strict dating rules, all his fears, and all the reasons he'd always be single. She saw him. The real him. And Nick wasn't sure he liked the view from her eyes.

"A deal is a deal." Her soft-spoken words felt like a punch to the stomach. This would never be a real relationship. He knew that. He was fine with it. But her detachment still stung.

The leather box seemed to float in the air between them. He stared at it. She stared at it. Like it was some kind of time bomb.

Finally, she took the box from his hand, opened it, and placed the ring on her finger. The damn thing fit perfectly. As if it were made for her. The light from the overhead fixture caught the stone, and she stared at the vintage-looking sapphire, studded with small diamonds all wrapped up in a platinum circle. Quite a score for his father—sentimental, too. No wonder his mom had wanted him to pawn it. Nick still remembered the day she'd given it to him to sell. He'd been fourteen. They'd needed the money, and he'd gone to sell it, but when he was standing there at the counter in the shop, he'd made the owner a deal instead. He swept that guy's floor for an entire year, but he'd let Nick keep the damn ring.

His gaze took in the sapphire sparkling on his fiancée's finger. He cleared his throat and tugged hard on his shirt collar. "The ring belonged to my mother."

Marianne looked up at him, her blue eyes a shade cooler, twisting the ring on her finger as if the decision to wear it was painful. "Don't worry. I'll make sure to return it in six weeks."

Chapter Eight

"Be a man of your word."
—mantelligence.com

Two hours into the event, it was clear Nick hated casino night. The spinning roulette wheel, the shuffling cards, the chiming slots—all of it. Especially Let It Ride poker; the game got under his skin like no other. Not surprising, given his father's choice to *let it ride* had cost Nick his childhood.

And tonight was worse than usual. He felt like a con man, a punk from the Heights all dressed up in a pricey suit, accessorized with a counterfeit fiancée to impress the high rollers. He took a pull from his beer. At least the money flying out of everyone's pockets would finance the dream of more than one kid from Brooklyn, a charitable cause he wholeheartedly supported.

If his partnership bid wasn't on the line, he'd clock in an hour's worth of requisite schmooze and get the hell out before the pulse of the makeshift casino grew unbearable. Already on edge, he wanted to take his fiancée home and put together a few more pieces of the puzzle, maybe play a game of Truth or Dare, use the mask he'd saved from Friday night to take her on a blind tour of her body. Oh yeah, Nick had definite plans. He took a short pull of his Heineken to cool down and scanned the room for Marianne, finding her sitting next to his boss happily schooling him in the art of blackjack.

Nick never bet—ever. He'd occasionally double down on darts with Charlie over a beer or two. But otherwise, he steered clear. The lure of the games was lost on him.

His fiancée, however, was on a roll.

He took a second pull of his beer and watched her at the table, expertly managing his boss with her reserved charm and apparent card-playing skills. In terms of saving his ass—so far, so good. He had to give it up to his sister, she'd found him the perfect temporary girl.

Emphasis on temporary. She might be his fantasy cake girl, even be wearing his sapphire ring, but that didn't change his DNA. Love wasn't his game. If he were smart, he'd remember that fact.

As if aware of his internal debate, Marianne turned and smiled reassuringly in his direction, all prim and sweet, a decided contrast to the dazzling sweater and the pink satin dress that hugged her hourglass figure. No doubt about it, Marianne was playing the role of fiancée to perfection, attentive to his boss, doe-eyed when she looked at him.

Completely believable.

Exactly what he needed her to be. So why the hell did Nick feel so unsettled?

"Enjoying the view there, bro?" Drew Evans asked, arriving at the exact wrong moment, drinking his usual Scotch, making his usual trouble. "She's pretty hot. Need another drink?"

"No." *And keep your eyes to yourself, you son of a bitch.* He raised his beer, which was full save a couple of sips. "I'm good."

"Not as good as your fiancée." Nick shot him a glare that told him to shut the hell up, and Evans took a half step back. "Take it easy. I'm not moving in on your action, although props to you for finding a woman like her on such short notice." Nick's hands balled into fists at his sides to keep from going all Brooklyn on Evan's ass. His temper had its limits, a fact Evans ignored. "You scored, Nick," he continued, waving his drink at the card table, "looks like your fiancée is quite the advantage player. Makes you wonder."

His jaw clenched defensively. Evans was an asshole, but the guy wasn't stupid. *An advantage player.* Nick had been thinking the exact same thing. Not that he'd let Evans know his usual running commentary hit its mark.

He took a sip of the Heineken. "A skillful use of mathematical advantage isn't illegal, you ought to know that," Nick said, his tone as chilled as a Monte Carlo martini. "There is an attorney underneath this high-priced suit."

"But not a partner." Evans's smile did not reach his eyes. A round of applause exploded around the blackjack table. His colleague cocked a dark eyebrow. "Better keep an eye on your fiancée and her shuffle-tracking skills. Never know what other secrets she keeps."

Watching Evans walk away, Nick felt an invisible band tighten around his chest. The truth was, he felt disquieted by

Marianne, by her satin dress, her numbers-based gambling talent, and yes, her secrets. His fiancée was more like him than he'd imagined, and while a buttoned-up cardigan girl wasn't his type, a table runner with a penchant for sequins and pop-out cakes? That woman sounded like fun. His eyes caught her gaze. Her hand fluttered to her throat, and the ring sparkled under the casino lights. *Too much fun.*

The dealer threw down another card. She swiveled on the green velvet chair, all innocent blue eyes and killer legs. Yeah, his fiancée had her secrets, secrets that were kind of sexy. He'd figure them out. But secrets were for later. Tonight, he had a partnership to win.

Nick cruised over to the gaming table. Marianne glanced at Dan's cards and pursed her lips. His boss stayed, she took the hit, and won the hand with a total of twenty.

"The firm is acting as the house tonight, Dan. Don't let her take too much of your money," he said, offering his boss a firm handshake. "She's a bit of a card shark."

A blush colored Marianne's skin as he bent to brush a kiss across her cheek. "Maybe I need to cash in my chips before my luck runs out."

"Nonsense," Dan said, with an encouraging smile. "All of tonight's proceeds go to charity, so I'm happy to be bested. What about you, Nick?" His boss turned his sharp gaze in his direction. "Ready to lose a little money for a good cause?"

Offering up his most polished smile, Nick said, "I'm not much of a gambler, but my donation will be on your desk in the morning."

"Glad to hear it," he said, before lowering his voice in side commentary. "She's a real sweetheart, a serious asset, too, even made Bill Jeffers chuckle, and I've not seen the man laugh in nearly fifteen years. If you don't marry her, I will."

Across the gaming table, a stack of chips fell, and a slightly drunken junior partner called out, "Let's see you kiss her, Nick."

His boss protested, but the rally cry of his colleagues grew louder. Five-hundred-dollar chips were tossed in his direction as his coworkers laid down odds on the length of the kiss, a few hashing out side bets should Nick fail to deliver. Hell, even Elvis sporting full jewel-encrusted attire and plenty of charisma got in on the action, breaking out in an off-key version of "A Little Less Conversation."

What could he do?

As the cheers rained down, Nick held up his hands in mock surrender and turned toward Marianne. A shy smile edged across her features as his hands curved around her waist. He bent his head and whispered, "What's the probability of me kissing you in front of all these people?"

She looked up at him from beneath her lashes. "Well, given that's it's for such a good cause, I'd say the event-to-outcome ratio is 100 percent."

Just what he needed to hear.

Nick took her face into his hands, brushed his thumb across her already pink cheek and kissed her, forgetting all about the chips and the wager. Hell, the whole partnership event was a memory, distant to the feel of her in his arms. Her lips parted, and his tongue dipped inside. She tasted like some sweet pineapple and rum concoction, tropical and exotic, a far cry from prim and proper. He felt no boundaries, temporary or otherwise, no barriers at all, save the edge of the table. All he wanted was to continue being lost in her kiss.

Without a thought in his head, he pressed her back against the table's green felt edge, eager to continue his pursuit of her mouth, the incredible feel of her, the luscious taste. No doubt about it now—she was his cake girl. And if he had his way later tonight, he'd show her how much she thrilled him. A stack of chips scattered onto the table, but who cared about blackjack? Nick didn't care about anything except kissing this woman.

As for the rest of it…

Let the chips fall where they may.

The dealer cleared his throat. Nick broke the kiss slowly, unconcerned that half the partnership was staring. Hell, the other half was cheering, and he didn't mind that, either. He pulled back another inch and grinned down at her, dazed and pretty, her new glasses askew. Funny how he'd never considered glasses sexy before. But on Marianne, it all worked. His smile deepened, and he reached out to straighten the damn things.

Nick knew he should move away, say their goodbyes, call it a night. Instead, he kept looking at her, his brain circling around the same three thoughts. One, he was engaged to a woman whose kiss had him thinking about sleepovers and back-to-back dates during football season. Two, the success of his entire career depended on her—at least for the next six weeks. And three, the woman had secrets.

Card-counting, cake-jumping, potentially, *career-busting* secrets.

And for some damned reason, he was still thinking sleepovers.

Chapter Nine

"The body is meant to be seen, not all covered up."
— *Marilyn Monroe*

That *kiss*.

Tucked into the corner of the living room's leather sectional, Marianne flipped through the massive, swirling universe of late night television in search of a classic movie, anything to keep from dwelling on the sweetness of Nick's lips on hers. She'd made a beeline for the bedroom after the party, but now she couldn't sleep—again—so she was channel-surfing in the living room.

She'd wanted a Marilyn movie, but since Nick didn't get the classic film channel, she'd have to settle for *The Big Bang Theory* or a midnight viewing of *Body Heat*. Wicked. Seductive. In line with her goal of becoming more sexually adventurous.

She clicked on the film and tried not to think too much

about the man on the pullout next door, all sleepy-eyed and naked. She swallowed hard, certain Nick slept naked. She snuck a peek at the door to his office.

Gloriously naked. She shoved aside an impulse to renegotiate the *no sex inside the relationship* part of their deal and settled against the buttery soft leather couch, determined to relax. Ever since her father's incarceration, she'd been unable to sleep. Ambien. Lunesta. Chardonnay. Nothing seemed to keep her thoughts from racing. Certainly knowing her fiancé was naked a few feet away didn't help. At least she had popcorn for a distraction. She ripped open the bag.

"Are you an insomniac as well as a card shark?"

Marianne drew in a startled breath, and her hands flew to her heart, sending popcorn flying into the air. A self-conscious laugh bubbled up from her chest. "You scared me."

"I'm sorry," he said, their words overlapping.

He took a step toward the couch at the same moment she stood to manage the popcorn situation and—bam—her body slammed smack-dab into The Great Wall of Nicholas.

Her gaze locked onto his perfectly defined deltoids, causing her brain to stop. Literally stop. In its tracks. No thoughts. No cranial activity. What. So. Ever. She blinked twice, or maybe several times, forcing her eyes to focus, but all she saw was the broad scope of his carry-me-to-bed-and-kiss-me-breathless shoulders.

Nick crouched to gather up the popcorn collected at her feet and tossed the stray kernels onto the coffee table. He looked up at her smiling, all rumpled and barefoot and gorgeous. "Or maybe you're simply addicted to old movies?"

Addicted. Oh, she was rapidly growing addicted to something, and it wasn't Ambien.

Or old movies.

Her knees gave out, and she collapsed onto the edge of the sectional, the unexpected movement causing the tie at the neckline of her Victorian-style nightie to fall open, revealing her curves to the silver moonlight streaming in through the windows.

Instinctively, she reached up to retie the straps, but noting how his surprised gaze turned heated before coasting from the open neckline to the floor, she released them. If she wasn't going to stop thinking about that kiss, then she may as well do something about it. She wanted more. Starting. Now. She raised both hands into the air. "Guilty on both counts, movies and insomnia."

Her inner siren was ready to play.

Leaving her neckline undone, she dropped her hands into her lap and leaned back against the corner of the couch. Guilty? Definitely, she thought, biting down hard on her lower lip, amazed at her new ability to flirt so freely.

He was close enough to kiss again, and wearing only a thin, V neck T-shirt and a pair of delicious, low-riding pajama bottoms. It was practically all she could do not to tug on the waistband of those pants and bring him tumbling down on top of her. *So go for it,* the husky voice of her inner seductress whispered, *please go for it.*

Her eyes dipped lower, past the top button to where the airy cotton stretched across the smooth skin of his muscular hips and thighs. What she wouldn't give to be that cotton right now. She slammed her eyes shut and her hands balled into fists to keep from reaching out to touch him. He was just so gorgeous. Crazy gorgeous in a way that caused her toes to tingle and her palms to itch with the need to run across his naked skin.

When her eyes fluttered open for another peek, he was easing all six feet and several inches of his body onto the comfy sofa. The cushion dipped under his weight, and she slid closer. Her heart beat triple time against her ribcage. Why did he have to sit so close, close enough to cause her mind to focus on the warmth emanating from his perfectly toned body? Oh yes, counselor, guilty on all counts. She pressed both hands to her cheeks. He wasn't even naked, and she was thinking about kicking their deal to the curb.

"Is this *Body Heat*?" Picking up the remote, he clicked up the volume, his eyes narrowing on the images moving across the screen. He glanced back at her, and her brows raised above the glasses in an unspoken question. "Nope. Not a movie buff. But I love Kathleen Turner."

"Really?" she said, surprised to learn his taste ran toward the curvy, smoky-voiced actress.

Nick lowered his chin and shot her a look that said, *Are you kidding me?* "Young Kathleen Turner in that lacy nightgown with the strap halfway down." His mischievous gaze drifted to the neckline of her sheer cotton nightie before returning to catch hers. "A sexual goddess."

Marianne swallowed hard. "A sexual goddess?" Right now, she wanted to be a sexual goddess more than anything in the world. Anything.

"But that's not the only reason I think she's great in this movie." With an air of casual ease and comfort, he reached across her body to grab the bag of popcorn. "She's downright sexy, sure, but she's got this air of bold confidence, too." He peeked inside the bag and grabbed a handful of popcorn. "She's the one running the game. Kind of like you tonight."

She glanced up at him from beneath her lashes. "Like me?"

A knowing smile creased his handsome face. "Honey, don't even try to pretend you weren't running the blackjack table tonight. I've been around enough gamblers to know when someone's managing the game." He tossed a few pieces of popcorn into the air and caught them in his mouth, consecutively, one, two, three. "Where'd you learn to count cards?"

Interesting. She'd been bold and stepped up her game with the nightgown, but he was holding back, playing it cool and casual and attorney-like. *Like she was about to get busted.*

Smoothing out the line of her nightie with her palm, she looked over at him and feigned innocence. "I don't count cards."

Another smile. "Honey, you ran the table like a Monte Carlo showgirl conning the sharks out of their cash. Don't pretend you didn't read the cards."

Honey? Oh, he was angling for information, all right, but she took the bait and tilted closer, drawn into the orbit of his smile, unable to deny the thrill of an endearment on his lips. "I was not like some sexy Monte Carlo showgirl."

He slipped a few more pieces of popcorn into his mouth and chewed. Her gaze locked onto his lips. "But you *were* reading the cards." The don't-even-try-to-play look on his face made her bare toes curl into the soft leather cushions. "C'mon, tell me your secrets."

"My secrets?" She tucked a strand of hair behind her

ear. "I don't keep secrets."

"No?" For a long moment he held her eyes, one corner of his lips pulled up in mischief.

"Tell me your secrets," he said in a voice that turned her inside out. "*All your secrets.*"

No sense even trying to resist the pull of that voice, not when he was talking about secrets and sitting so close and wearing low-riders she wanted to ease off with her teeth. The confession tumbled out of her in a rush. "I counted the cards."

Nick made a victorious sound at the back of his throat and pointed at her with the popcorn bag. "I knew it."

She snuggled deeper into the cushions. "There's nothing sexy about counting cards."

"A girl who can count cards—are you kidding me?" He dropped another smile on her and tossed the bag onto the coffee table. "Sexier than a showgirl." Empty now, his hands moved along the edge of the cushion, inches away from the hem of her nightgown. "Any other equally hot secrets?"

"I told you I don't keep secrets."

He looped a strand of her hair around his index finger and tilted forward until he was close enough to whisper. "Are you sure about that, Cake Girl?" Her eyes widened as his gaze took a southern detour from her lips. "Whisper 'Happy Birthday' in my ear." He reached for the half-tied strap at her neckline and tugged her forward. "I dare you."

She shook her head. "I never played Truth or Dare."

"Well, then, let me teach you."

With a smile that in all probability was going to cost her way more than her secrets, he inched even closer, his per-fectly shaped mouth just a breath away. "Truth or dare, you are the girl who jumped out of my birthday cake in that silver dress."

"But the movie…" she said in a low, husky voice.

"Truth or dare."

Eyes locked onto his, a dizzying buzz ran through her system, and she dared to whisper, "Truth."

"You want to kiss me again. Truth or dare?"

Tell him the truth, her inner temptress beckoned, *tell him the truth.* "Better take the dare."

In a movement so sweet, so seductively tender, she almost forgot about the game as he brushed a strand of hair away from her cheek. "I dare you to kiss me."

The challenge in his voice made her dizzier still, and a play-by-the-rules kind of girl, she offered up a brief kiss — enough to satisfy his dare, but no more than his birthday kiss.

His eyes half closed, his lips clung to hers, unwilling to let go. "God, you are so sexy."

She shook her head in slow, heartfelt denial. "I'm so not sexy."

"Marianne, I don't know why you feel that way, but I could not disagree more." He bent to kiss the edge of her collarbone, and the feel of his lips on her skin sent her senses reeling way past probabilities and correlations. "Why did you run from my birthday party?" His gaze sought hers, and she looked into his midnight blue eyes. "Didn't you know how badly I wanted to kiss you again? The girl in the cake, the perfect birthday gift."

Any second the spell would end, but until then, she breathed in the warmth of his skin, his deep, masculine scent, as fresh and thrilling as Central Park in spring. "I don't know…maybe I thought if you knew it was me, the 'quintessential good girl,' you wouldn't want me." *There*. She'd said it. Her emotional moment of truth.

"Oh honey, trust me, I want you." His hands reached up to frame her face, and his mouth moved toward her lips to kiss her. The kind of kiss she'd wanted all along. She didn't move. She didn't think she was breathing. She was simply suspended in the moment, waiting for his kiss, knowing that this kiss would change everything. Maybe not for Nick, but for her. And she wanted it, wanted it more than anything. Her lips parted in an invitation he readily accepted, diving in to kiss her, gently at first, increasing the depth and pressure with each soft moan of encouragement.

He pulled his lips away slowly, his thumbs caressing their edges. "God, I love those little sounds you make…drive… me…crazy."

That voice.

Drive…me…crazy. Oh, she knew the feeling. Her hands twisted in the hair at the back of his neck, dragging him closer, returning his kiss with unfamiliar need. She loved the feel of his rumpled, less-than-tidy hair threaded through her fingers, the rough texture of his five-o'clock shadow against her skin.

He pulled away slightly, but stayed close enough that she could feel his breath on her cheek, the soft cotton of his T-shirt tickling the skin at her open neckline. He edged her glasses away from her face and eased her back against the soft leather, reaching past her to set her glasses on an end table. The spectacular play of muscles in his forearms and biceps sent heat racing through her body. "I wanted you that first night." He reached into the pocket of his low-riders and withdrew the turquoise mask she'd left behind in the bar. "And I want you right now."

She gasped at the sight of her disguise and fisted his T-shirt in her hands.

"Close your eyes and let me show you just how incredibly sexy you are."

"Nick…"

"Close. Your. Eyes." His gaze locked onto hers, he unfolded the mask…slowly…like a seduction, and her eyes drifted shut. He slipped the mask on her face and tied the ribbon at the back of her neck. Every fiber of her body pulsated in anticipation, aware of the gentle movement of his strong hands as they caressed her shoulders, skimming the outside of her arms, detouring into the subtle inlet of her waist. "Tell me if you want to stop."

A pleading moan escaped her. The heck with the deal. "I don't want to stop."

His hands blazed a trail across her ribcage, moving across the curve of her hips and stomach to the apex of her thighs. She moaned as he touched her. Exposed and willing, her lips sought his. Soft, sexy whimpers rose from the back of her throat. "Kiss me," she said.

His lips covered hers, not searching, not sweet, but exquisitely rough, diving into the depths of her mouth.

He moved one knee between her legs, and his fingers found the hem of her nightgown. "Do you know how sexy you are?"

"No," she whispered.

"Do you want me to show you?" he asked, moving the fabric higher, drifting past her knees to reveal the tender skin of her upper thighs. With her eyes closed, the sensations were magnified. "Or do you want me to stop?"

"I want you to show me."

She felt a rustle of movement, then his teeth nipped at one of her nipples through the filmy fabric of her nightgown. Instinctively, her body arched against him and her head fell back in an open invitation to explore her body more completely. Her body trembled, responding to his every bite and touch. He circled the edge of her nipple, first with his palm, then with the tips of his fingers, pinching and tweaking as his tongue licked and kissed her aching nipple though the cotton, switching his ministrations between each breast until she thought she might combust.

Eyes closed, she felt his warmth against her skin, teasing her, misdirecting her with his breath and his voice, causing her body to arch in search of him only to be surprised when his mouth found a new, undiscovered place to tease and caress. Her nails dug into his shoulders, and when he nipped the throbbing peaks again, she gasped at the pleasure and pain of his touch. "Nick, please," she whispered. "I can't wait any more."

Beneath the hem of her nightgown, his fingers blazed a hot trail over her thighs, across her stomach, toward her wet center. She was ready, hot and wet and waiting to feel his touch inside her. Two fingers slid under the lacy edge of her panties to trace her opening. God, she felt so sexy and free. He pressed his fingers deep inside.

Every touch sent her reeling into dangerous territory. He flicked her clit with his thumb and she felt raw need stretch across her features. Her body shuddered as his fingers circled her core, easing in and out of her. Time melted away as he worked the most sensitive parts of her body, driving her straight to the edge of desperation. All she could think about was him and this wondrous new sense of pleasure and adventure.

This is what it felt like to be appreciated by a man. To have him touch her until she was hot and desperate and pleading. This was what she'd been missing.

Her inner siren was officially in the building.

In his home.

In his arms.

As his fingers continued to circle her, his free hand peeled the nightie off her shoulders, allowing his lips to work their way across her naked breasts, tasting her heated skin, stopping only to hear her moan and cry out with agonized desire, before his kiss traveled farther, upward and across her collarbone, burrowing in her neck, licking at her earlobe, until finally moving over to her begging lips.

He kissed her breathless, breaking away to whisper, "Do you want me to stop?"

"No, I want you to make me come."

He froze for a moment, then his hand retreated to grab hold of the panties and tug them down. He pushed the nightgown over her hips until she was half naked, her breath coming hot and heavy and so, so desperate.

Marianne didn't need to take off the mask to know she'd been set free. Only one person in the world knew how to release her desire this way, her temporary fiancé, the one whose hands were causing her body to tremble. She turned her head and shut her eyes, needing to block out the truth.

"Open your eyes."

Responding to the sensual command in his voice, her eyes fluttered open. The slits in the mask limited her range of vision, but her gaze unerringly found his.

"I want to see you when I make you come apart in my arms."

"Nick." His name tumbled from her lips. "Please."

He smiled down at her with the sweetest look in his eyes. "I want to prolong this moment, right now. I want to tease you and breathe you in."

A desperate whimper hitched in the back of her throat as his fingers buried inside her, demanding the release her body was so ready to give.

She trembled as the new and tantalizing sensations running through her built to a fever pitch. Her heart pounded out a crazy rhythm as he coaxed the rise and fall of her body, building the intensity of feeling inside her, daring her to resist until all she wanted to do was scream with the need for release. Her hands curled into the muscles of his shoulder. She was ready, so ready. God, she'd never known she could feel like this.

He bent his head and kissed her through it, leading her body into and out of the series of explosions, murmuring her name as the pieces of her insides scattered and reformed like an image in a kaleidoscope. "Totally sexy," he said, his lips lingering against her mouth.

And, for that moment, Marianne believed him.

Chapter Ten

"Live in the present, but plan for the future."
— mantelligence.com

Maybe it was the glasses.

Nick sat behind the desk in his home office, his fingers tapping out the rhythm of John Coltrane's *My Favorite Things*, wondering how the hell he'd gotten so caught up in the moment last night. The normal logic of his rules and his partnership plan and his need for short-term had booked a flight to Miami Beach, and now that he'd crossed the off-limits line, a slew of new things topped his list of favorites.

Like his fiancée lying back against the leather cushions, all soft lips and steamed-up horn-rims, skin flushed and heated, blue eyes filled with a combination of innocence and unconstrained desire. *Those* favorites. He'd figured out the puzzle. Solved the mystery. Marianne was the cake girl. Now it was time to move on—like always.

Except that he couldn't get her off his damn mind. Which was crazy. He was a man with rules. A man used to a different woman every other week.

Yeah, had to be the glasses. Why else would he feel so... protective? Well, protective and horny as hell. Devil damned if he understood it, but those specs were a major turn-on. Maybe it was some kind of librarian fantasy. He made a low sound in the back of his throat and shifted in the chair, suddenly uncomfortable in his casual, work-at-home jeans.

A cold shower might keep him from thinking about the glasses. Except Little Miss Slip-Aside-My-Cardigan-and-Take-Me was down the hall. If he laid eyes on her, he'd strip away the cardigan and the glasses—and whatever else she was wearing. Strip it away slowly, caressing the line of her spine, until his fingers tangled in the hair at the back of her neck and tugged her head back to gaze into those baby blues, so deep and vulnerable, bright with desire...

His hands slammed down on the armchair.

What the hell was wrong with him?

No matter how much heat was between them, he wasn't a love kind of guy and she needed a love kind of man, a man willing to move to Connecticut, crank out the unachievable 2.5 kids and drive a freaking Prius. Not some wayward guy from Brooklyn zip-lining through relationships dictated by rules like *No Sundays during football season.* Not that there was anything wrong with rules and zip lines. He liked rules and zip lines. Liked them a lot.

But he liked Marianne, too, and when his sister found out how far he'd let things go with her friend—and in the space of a few days—she'd make him pay. Better to rein it in now. Like he had last night, when Marianne had wanted to reciprocate. He'd known then—as he did now—if his dick had made it out of his pants that he wouldn't have stopped.

He'd never manage to honor a promise to a woman like Marianne. Smart, sweet, sexy as a summer night of jazz at the Blue Note. A total surprise, the kind of woman who deserved a good man.

But not the kind of woman for him.

Nick rolled the leather chair away from his desk. Marriage. Children. He'd never wanted all that, not after witnessing the devastation of his father's exit. But here he was, a first-rate workaholic sitting in his home office on a Wednesday afternoon thinking about making more sexy trouble with Marianne.

He'd started this charade to get a partnership, and now he was stuck with a fiancée who he was wildly attracted to and it was all he could do to keep from thinking about what would happen after his six weeks were up.

Listening to her move around his place made him wish he were a better man, a man capable of commitment. But there were no exceptions for a guy like him.

The office door creaked open, and he looked up to see Marianne standing there, her slender hand wrapped around the knob. She leaned forward, and her cleavage dipped just enough to give him a glimpse of what he'd enjoyed last night. *Six weeks, six survivable weeks,* he'd thought when she moved in. Now he was wondering how he'd survive when the time was up. "New dress?" he asked.

Balancing on the doorknob, she swayed forward slightly as her palm smoothed the cotton jersey over the curve of her hip. "Do you like it?"

Like it? He fucking *loved* it.

The tentative tone in her voice as she asked compelled his gaze upward from her hips to the half smile touching her lips. Everything about her was so unintentionally seductive. He imagined the seduction was unintentional anyway. But maybe not. Maybe his newfangled, not-so-buttoned-up fiancée was looking for a little afternoon delight. His dick twitched inside his denims. If so, he was ready to accommodate.

Nick bit back a groan. When did his prim fiancée turn into a vixen, all wrapped up in the kind of sweet floral dress that simply begged to be unraveled? Damn, he'd never been jealous of a dress before, but there was obviously a first time for everything. "I definitely like."

"Good...okay...well..." She chewed on her lower lip, seeming to debate her next move, a move he could only dream included her lifting the skirt over her knees and wrapping those legs around him as he tutored her in the joys of up-against-the-wall sex. "Guess I'll see you later."

Nick shot out of his chair fast enough to leave it spinning behind him. "Wait a second. Where are you going?"

"The movies."

In that dress?

"With a friend?" Nick hung his thumbs on the belt loops of his jeans.

Or maybe a date? Because their engagement had rules— no reneging on the timeline, no dating, no outside relationships, and *no outside sex*. But she had secrets. He shook his head. No, skirting the rules didn't seem like Marianne's style. She seemed by-the-book. Then again, she'd kept the whole cake girl thing hush-hush. And there was the matter of the smoking hot dress. He ran a hand across the stubble on his jaw as a realization smacked him in the face.

He was jealous. *Jealous*. And not only of the dress.

In an obvious stall tactic, she readjusted her glasses against the bridge of her nose. "No…not a friend."

Nick kept his voice casual. "Because I can finish up. We can close the blackouts and watch a movie at home." *At home? Had he really said, at home? What was happening to him?*

Marianne gave him the sweetest, sexiest glance from beneath her dark lashes. Damn, he could get used to that look. "Like last night?"

Reaching for the fabric belt tied neatly at her waist, he tugged her a little closer. "I can always behave…unless you're interested in an encore," he teased, enjoying the blush on her cheeks. "What do you say? No ticket, no sticky floors, no mouth breathers wedged into the next seat." *His tongue licking her heated skin along the way to her core.*

"I can't."

"Why not?" he asked, untying the sweet bow. "If you don't have another date."

Marianne slapped his hand away and retied the bow in a double knot. "Not that I expect you to know everything about me…"

He waggled his eyebrows. "I know a helluva lot more about you after last night."

Like the fact that she made more unabashedly sexy noises than any woman he'd ever been with. Like how much her sounds turned him on. Made him crave more.

"I volunteer as an accountant for the Lincoln Center Film Society. *And God Created Woman* is playing at the Francesca Beale. Normally, I'm not a fan of French cinema, but…" She wrinkled her nose, and Nick fought back the impulse to lean close and kiss away her displeasure. "But I was wondering if maybe you would like to go with me?"

Born and raised in Brooklyn on B movies and HBO, Nick suspected a film club wasn't his speed, and he ought to be working, but looking into her vulnerable blue eyes as she worked up the nerve to go all Sadie Hawkins on him made him want to forgo his work and spend the rest of the late afternoon at the movies.

A smile broke across his face. "On one condition."

"Only one? Your negotiation skills are slipping, counselor."

"Back-row seats." An adorable *V* formed between her eyebrows, and he realized how much he was starting to enjoy her trademarks. He reached for her and, rather than swivel away, her hips swayed a little closer. He splayed his hands across the top of her heart-shaped ass, pressing his advantage. "Perfect place to show you exactly why God created women."

She spun out of his arms and strolled over to the door, tossing him a smile over her shoulder. "You are a bad boy."

He shifted in his jeans and followed, watching her backside move in that curve-hugging dress. Oh, yeah, Nick planned on being a very bad boy and, while his fiancée hadn't agreed to the back-row seats, she definitely hadn't said no.

"Brigitte Bardot's got nothing on you, honey." Nick held her hand as they walked along Spring Street toward the French bakery on the corner, and the feeling of his fingers laced with hers made Marianne feel as if she were walking on clouds rather than cobblestone.

Nick opened the door of Le Minuit Café and a trill of wind chimes announced their arrival. With his hand at her back, he directed her to an intimate corner table for two. A group of thirty-somethings dressed for ladies' night out looked over at Nick, eyes flashing like they'd like to wrap him up in to-go paper and run off with him. But there were no disbelieving looks, no expressions of disdain floating in her direction. She slipped into the bistro chair Nick held for her, smoothed the fabric of her wrap dress over her knees, and wondered if she might successfully compete with Brigitte tonight. After the back row of the movie, Marianne was on fire and ready to take her inner siren for a spin.

Nick leaned in close. "Know what you'd like?"

Oh, she knew what she liked. She liked Nick. His eyes, his smile, his hands on her skin. "I'd like a Frangelico please… and for dessert…" she said, letting the hint of a flirtatious smile touch her lips and her eyes drift to meet his, "surprise me."

His gaze fell to her mouth, and Marianne could tell from his expression how badly he wanted to kiss her. In the past, she would've looked away, all fidgety and uncomfortable under his masculine gaze. But not tonight.

He tucked a piece of hair behind her ear, dropped a kiss on her forehead and said, "Consider yourself surprised."

Watching him walk away, Marianne felt a wonderful buzz race along her spine. He wore his jeans like a man who was comfortable in his own skin, as if he wore nothing at all, a thought that sent her pulse rocketing through the skylight above her. His black button-down shirt stretched across his broad shoulders and tapered down the strong line of his back. And he was her date.

From across the bistro, her gaze ate him up as if he was her own private adventure waiting to happen. Not that it got hotter or more adventurous than the back of the movie theater. Her eyes closed remembering how he'd slipped his fingers under the hem of her dress. How he'd taken his sweet time, tracing circles on her ticklish knees, inching his way up along the inside of her thigh, slipping his finger inside her panties to find her already wet. The way he'd touched her, his eyes straight ahead as if glued to the screen. As if he wasn't driving her to the very limits of desire, easing away his fingers as her body grew taut, refusing to let her crash, reveling in his control over her body. She'd gripped the arms of the theater's red velvet seats and bit down hard on her bottom lip to keep from crying out in the darkened, half-filled room. The excitement of being surrounded by strangers, knowing at any moment they could get caught, had turned her on like the lights on the front marquee.

Marianne had never imagined that kind of excitement, and the truth was, being wild and reckless had felt good. Nick had showed her the thrill of being bad. He'd left his mark on her body and soul. Classic movies would never be the same.

Now, she hoped to return the favor. She'd done a cost-benefit analysis of the situation and had made her decision. Tonight, she planned to step it up. She'd downloaded a copy of *A Girl's Guide to Becoming a Vixen,* a best-selling manual that offered step-by-step instructions designed to achieve maximum seduction success. More than anything, Marianne wanted a chance to intoxicate him the way he'd intoxicated her.

"Dessert," Nick said, returning to the table with her hazelnut liqueur and a heavenly looking chocolate éclair that was worlds away from her usual low-carb ricotta cheesecake.

She glanced up at him from beneath her lashes. "You are corrupting me, Nick."

"Honey, I'm just getting started."

Her sentiments exactly, she thought, as he strode over to the bar to pick up his coffee.

A minute or two later, settled across from the man of her literal dreams, she felt a blush steal across her cheeks. Thinking about seducing him was one thing, but acting on it was more difficult than she'd calculated. Sure, she'd studied the techniques in the manual, but there was no perfect formula. She smoothed the hem of her dress with her fingertips. Ready or not...

Step one: eye contact. Shooting for bombshell, she leaned forward and looked into the depths of his midnight blue eyes. "Did you enjoy the movie?"

"Not my usual. I'm more an action guy. Steve McQueen, Vin Diesel and *The Furious Seven*, but I enjoyed being there with you, seeing you in action."

His gaze dipped to the slight *V* of her dress, and a wave of heat swept across her face as her nipples pushed against the soft fabric. There was no cardigan to hide her physical response, but with Nick, she felt less and less like hiding.

He'd been so wonderful, accompanying her to the film, indulging her as she gave him a tour of the theater, listening intently to her discuss the joys of being a small part of the film restoration process. He'd made her feel seen and appreciated in a way she'd never felt before, lost in all his glorious male attention, both before and during the movie.

Nick looked over at her and smiled a shockingly wicked smile. "Might want to unwrap that dress later tonight."

Steps two: use touch. "How much later?" she asked, running her fingers up one of his muscular, denim-clad thighs. She moved another inch or two then glided back down to his knee before beginning her upward ascent to the Promised Land again. She didn't have the patience that he'd exhibited in his under-the-skirt theater torture, but she had the wherewithal to follow that second directive of step two: *move slowly—it enhances the sensory perception.* She could testify to that firsthand thanks to Nick. And she had every intention of returning the favor. She heard his intake of breath and eased back slowly to take in his heated expression. His wicked smile deepened. "Are you trying to seduce me, woman?"

Step three: express desire. "Sounds promising."

He reached out and placed his hand on top of hers, effectively ending any further attempt at a slow seduction. "Oh, I think you know exactly how promising."

Step four: hold back a little. A bit of mystery goes a long way. "What do you mean?" she asked, her eyes wide behind her glasses as she eased her hand away and picked up the dessert. His eyes darkened, and in a move more brazen than she'd ever attempted, ever even considered before this moment, Marianne held his gaze and took a leisurely bite of the luscious éclair. The sweet confection was so much better than the low-carb kind she practically moaned aloud, never imagining she could feel this way, so daring and delicious. *Wow, that was really good.*

Without another research-filled thought, she took a second yummy bite of the pastry and a bit of the white cream clung to her lips.

"Let's get out of here." Before she could lick it away, Nick reached out and wiped the sugary filling from her mouth with his thumb. *"Now."*

Nick planned to make her pay for the move with the éclair.

Hell, she'd taken one bite of the creamy dessert and he'd been ready to pull her into the back of the place for a quickie. Except a hurried encounter wasn't going to be enough for him. The walk from the café across the street was the last thing he'd be rushing.

His hand low on her back, he ushered Marianne through the lobby, glad that Max was home for the night and he could forgo the lengthy niceties. He kept his cool as he guided her into the elevator and to the door of the condo. Inside, he wrapped his arm around her waist and pulled her toward him as he fell back against the door. Nipping at her earlobe, he slid his palms up her hips and stomach and cupped her breasts. Her nipples tightened and he flicked them gently, thrilled by the raspy moan of satisfaction that escaped her. Her head fell back, and he licked her throat, letting his hands roam her breasts, enticing soft, pleading whimpers from her lips. Damn, the sounds she made drove him wild. He kneaded the soft flesh beneath his hands, tweaking the pointed tips until she arched forward to fill his hands more completely. He felt crazed for the sound of her, the touch, the taste. Her ass pressed against his groin, and he released a low growl of need. His hands fell to her hips, and she turned in his arms, looking up at him like the world-class temptation she was.

He linked his fingers through hers and tugged her away from the door.

"Where are we going?" she asked in her hushed, sexy tone.

Nick glanced back at her, all disheveled and hot, the lace of her bra peeking from the tugged-away neckline.

"You'll see."

He walked through the living room, passed the hall that led to his bedroom, and cut straight into the office. Marianne's gaze fell on his desk, and she bit her lip as if contemplating the kind of damage they could do on top of it. Nick made a mental note to try that later, flung open the door of his closet, and walked her inside. He stepped toward her and she fell back against the third step. His hands on either side of her, Nick lowered his mouth to the low *V* of her dress and ran his tongue along the line of the exposed lace.

Marianne kicked off her shoes and slid her ass up to the next stair, letting his mouth dip lower, edging away the fabric of her dress and bra to reveal more heated skin. Her ass slid up another stair, and he followed her, his lips kissing the tops of her breasts, edging away the material with his chin. He pulled one rosy, pleading nipple into his mouth and sucked until her flesh was raw and throbbing, the way she'd come to enjoy.

"Oh, Nick," she sighed.

Time to move on. Releasing her, Nick entered the code for the lock and pressed open the door. He helped her onto the roof, took her hand, and led her to a hidden corner where a slatted porch swing hung from a secluded pergola surrounded by flowing ivy and fragrant, brightly colored flowers. In the distance, the city's lights blinked, dotting the twilight sky. He loved this time of day, the time between the rush of the day and the night's possibilities.

Her eyes twinkled over at him as he reached for the belt at her waist.

"Time to unwrap my birthday present."

"Belatedly," she said.

Thank God for private rooftop gardens. Nick smiled. "I'll take you as a present anytime, honey."

He pulled on the fabric and she turned, unwrapping the dress in the process. Finished, she stood in front of him, the dress gaping open to reveal her sweet, white lace bra and panties. His hands moved to his belt, but she stepped forward to still them. With her gaze locked onto his, her fingers worked the metal of the belt until it fell open. She undid the button at the waist, unzipped his jeans, and pressed her palm against the bulge in his briefs. He groaned, so ready.

Unable to wait, he dragged his jeans and underwear down and kicked them onto the flagstone. He drew her close, cradling her in his arms as he urged her to lie on the oversized, cushioned bench swing. She wrapped around his waist, clinging to him as he settled comfortably on top of her, one knee braced on the swing, the other on the ground.

A smile spread across his face, and he eased her panties over her hips enough to slide his fingers inside her. She was so slick and wet. His fingers worked her delicately, bringing her closer and closer to the edge. But he didn't let her come.

"Oh God," she whispered, her body straining for release.

"I want to be inside you, Marianne."

She fisted his collar and tugged him close. "Counselor, are you proposing an amendment to our agreement? I'm referencing article four—no sex for the duration of our agreement. Because I'd like to strike that from the contract."

Hell yes. He made a low sound in the back of his throat. "Consider it struck."

The stipulations he'd jotted down on the coffee shop napkin were already forgotten. In fact, he'd be shredding the damn thing first chance he got. Because tonight—and every night for the next five weeks—she was his girl, his fiancée, and he wanted to bury himself deep inside her and mark her as his own.

The dress cascaded over the edge of the swing as she bucked against his playing fingers, raising her hips in a series of small pleading movements. "Yes."

Nick didn't think it was possible to get any harder, but he was wrong, so very, very wrong. He slipped his fingers out of her, teasing her along the way before reaching back to drag his jeans close enough to slip a condom from his pocket. He balanced his body back onto the oversized swing. Eyes never leaving her, he pulled the condom over his aching erection. God, how he wanted her.

Everything about her thrilled him, her gentle curves, her warm scent, the longing in her husky voice as she sighed against his lips. Every fiber of his body pulsed, aware of every inch of her as he positioned his hips above her. Gripping the back of the swing, she wriggled her ass, and the panties fell past her knees to give him perfect access to her heat. He peeled them down her shapely legs.

Nick dropped a fervent, lingering kiss on her parted lips and circled her tongue with demanding strokes until her trembling body rose up to meet him, one arm braced against the back of the swing. He entered her slowly, allowing her to accept him. His free hand slid around her back to cradle her and grasp the curve of her ass, edging her hips higher. He drove into her slowly at first, increasing his rhythm as she slammed her hips upward. The movement of the swing and her rising body worked in concert to welcome him deep inside. But it wasn't enough.

A hand moved down the back of her thigh to the bend at her knee and looped under to tug open her killer legs. He plunged deeper, and she cried out, her hands tearing at his shirt before burying into the hair at the back of his neck.

"Nick!"

He slipped his tongue into her open mouth, moving and guiding her to the next level of want, pulling her body closer until no space separated their bodies, until he was deep inside her, as deep as he could go. Their bodies rocked together in time with the swing, his aching cock moving in and out of her, circling, thrusting, working her over until she moaned softly, a look of exquisite agony on her face.

He'd never wanted a woman with such intensity. "Don't hold back," he whispered against her cheek.

Her body arched forward, clenching all around him as she screamed his name. "Nick. Hells. Bells," she cried out, her nails digging into his shoulders through the thin cotton of his shirt. "I am coming…so hard…so hard."

Jesus, he was ready to join her. He buried his face in her shoulder and cried out her name. The rooftop felt like it was spinning. The city's lights and faraway sounds seemed to swirl around them as he came crashing down in a climax so pure, so full of release, he was struck again by his desire, no, his need, to do it again—and again.

Nick gathered her against him, wrapping her dress

around her to safeguard her naked skin against the slight chill in the air. He gazed down at her. As the sky darkened, the automatic twinkle lights strung from the pergola flickered into life, bathing her sweetly flushed face in a soft white glow. The swing gently rocked them back and forth, and he held her close in his arms. There was no doubt. This rooftop was officially his favorite place in New York. He pressed a kiss against her temple.

Marianne looked up at him. "Can we do that again?" Nick shifted his body to accommodate her request and the swing rocked backward. "Honey, you do not have to ask me twice."

Thank God they'd renegotiated the no sex inside the relationship *clause.*

Because Nick was about to double down.

Chapter Eleven

"What do I wear in bed? Why, Chanel No. 5, of course."
—Marilyn Monroe

Marianne woke up the next morning wearing Nick's half-buttoned black shirt, a pair of lacy white panties and nothing else. After a second round of rooftop sex, they'd wandered downstairs, and Nick had held her until they'd fallen asleep watching late night movies. Best of all, she'd slept the entire night. On the sectional. In the living room.

When was the last time she'd gotten nine hours of sleep on a perfectly modulated spring form mattress much less on a couch? Sometime before her dad's arrest? Before the dominatrix? Marianne wasn't sure. But she knew she owed her blissful sleep to Nick. The idea that her peaceful night had anything to do with spending it in a pair of strong arms rocked her to her soul. Yes, Nick had been her sexual crush, a fantasy, but now she was living in his house, kissing him until she was breathless, and sleeping through the night. And he was humming in the kitchen. *Humming*.

Not only was her inner bad girl awake and fully engaged, but her heart was following suit, foolishly unaware it was simply on loan for another thirty-six days.

She needed to be careful. While expanding her seductive horizons was breathtakingly liberating, at the end of the day, she was still a woman who wanted to find her happily-ever-after. And despite his midnight company and rooftop kisses, there were no fairy-tale endings with Nick Wright. She lifted the collar of his shirt and breathed in his warm, masculine scent. Better to enjoy the heat between them. Be sexy, be fun, be careful.

Except when the man of her dreams walked in carrying a breakfast tray, her ever hopeful heart skipped a beat and started dreaming of forever.

He let go a long, low whistle. "You look good wearing my clothes and nothing else."

"Not nothing else." She twisted her body into a pinup pose straight out of a Turner Cable classic and looked over at him. "I'm wearing panties."

A wicked smile creased his handsome, unshaven face, and the tray clattered onto the table. "We can definitely change that situation."

An exclamation bubbled up from her chest as he dove toward her, smiling. She grabbed a pillow and fought him off, the breath rushing out of her as she tumbled back against the corner of the sectional. He grabbed at his shirt—the one she was wearing—in a misguided attempt to stop her, but she landed a clean hit to his backside. He moved closer, but she continued to pummel his chest, shoulders, forearms. He reached behind her for a pillow to use as a shield, dodging her shots to the left and the right, grabbing for her pillow, finding instead the soft inside of her thigh. She let go a high-pitched protest and fell back against the couch as he tumbled on top of her, both of them laughing and out of breath.

He nodded at the tray on the coffee table. "Breakfast in bed, or rather, on the sectional. I didn't know what you liked so I brought you a little bit of everything…three tea options, orange juice, yogurt, two kinds of granola, scrambled eggs, French toast and a fruit cup—and me, of course." Another grin as he leaned in close. "But I already know you like me over easy."

A hint of a smile touched her lips. "Thank you. For the breakfast. And the over easy."

"You. Are. Welcome." He punctuated each word with a kiss that had her reaching for him, wondering if a little flirtation might mean more kissing, until…she saw the tension at the edges of his eyes. "And by the way, your mother called, and my sister told her we were engaged."

"She did what?" Her body snapped from happily relaxed to strung out like a tightrope. She shot up like a rocket, her tone tense and clipped. "I never planned to tell my family we were *engaged*. How did this even happen?"

Nick sat down next to her and rubbed at the back of his neck. "Apparently when you didn't answer your cell last night, your mom decided to call the Smart Cupid office…"

"Of course she did." Her head dropped into her open palms. *How humiliating.* A grown woman being tracked down by her mother.

He peeked through her fingers. "And we're supposed to be there tomorrow. By five."

"Tomorrow?" Her heart accelerated into a full-blown panic. "But the party isn't for another two weeks." *Tomorrow by five.* She wasn't ready. There were too many facts she hadn't told him yet...like the fact that she'd been engaged to a man whose taste in women ran to the kinky, or that her father had been recently incarcerated. "Did she call here? Did you talk to her?"

Nick scrubbed his face with both hands, looking like he was barely holding on to his cool. "Yes, she called here, wanting to congratulate us on the engagement, and you were sleeping—what the hell was I supposed to do? Hang up and pretend I'd moved to Siberia?

She drew in a shaky breath. "No, it's okay." *Don't freak out. Don't freak out. Don't freak out.* "What did you tell her?"

"First, I told her you've been busy having orgasms all over New York City."

She fisted her hands in his damned Yankees shirt. "Seriously, what did you say?"

"I told her we'd be there by five."

"You told her *what*?"

"What should I have said?" he asked with a trace of irritation in his voice. "Six weeks of engagement on my end and a commitment to your family event on yours—that was our deal."

"Yes, but...as my *date*, not my *fiancé*."

He held up his hands in a kind of mock surrender. "How was I supposed to know that?"

Hells bells, they were never going to be able to sell this one. She'd been engaged once before, but they'd dated for seven years and ended up a total disaster, so the likelihood of her making the same commitment eight months later was statistically improbable.

Hells.

Bells.

She leaped off the couch and beelined across the room. She needed to think, to recalculate. Better yet, she needed the next two weeks to master the sexy and work up the nerve to explain to Nick about her family and the party and the dominatrix. Now what was she supposed to do? Confess? What if he backed out?

Nick strode up behind her, put his hands on her shoulders, and she jumped. "Okay, you need to relax. We had a fantastic night last night, so let's not create any trouble this morning."

"Let's not create any trouble?" Her voice crept up an octave, and she whirled around to look at him. "Trust me, Nick, we are not ready for my family. Certainly not *tomorrow*. If you don't count the times we've literally bumped into each other at the office, we've really only known each other for six days—my mom will take one look at you and know you are so not my kind of guy."

Nick stared back at her. "Because I'm not the can't-wait-to-meet-your-mom type? Is that what you're implying? I'm not good enough to be that kind of guy?"

"Maybe." She bit down on her bottom lip but refused to back down. After all, he was a proven serial dater, and yes, they'd shared some fantastic sex, but that didn't mean he'd changed his tune to include commitment. "Yes."

Anger radiated off him. "You know what, Marianne? You're right. I'm not the Prius guy who wants to run out to the Hamptons to meet the mom. I'm the guy who likes a weekend commitment. Not a month or a year or a lifetime. But we made a deal, and I intend to stick to it, because I am *not* the kind of guy who bails. But don't think I'm all that thrilled about driving out to meet your family as your fiancé, a role that requires me to look like a man in love, rather than a man just along for the ride."

A small stab of pain shot through her. *"A man along for the ride?"* she repeated, stabbing at her glasses. After the last few nights, she'd actually started to imagine a happily-ever-after, but she should have known better. "That's dating to you, isn't it? *Going along for the ride."*

His eyes narrowed on her face, but he said nothing.

Her chin angled up a centimeter in a kind of dare. "Oh, I know all about your rules. No sleepovers, no back-to-back dates, some crazy stipulation about football—"

"Hey, now you're getting personal."

"But don't forget, Nick, *you* came to me looking for a fiancée and *your* sister spilled the beans to my family." Her fists formed into tight balls at her sides. "So don't blame me for the fact that you need to step up and act like a man capable of more than *going along for the ride."*

A charged silence grew between them, and Marianne wondered if she'd crossed the line. Not like she wasn't guilty. She hadn't filled him in on her ex or her dad or the domina-trix. For all he knew she could be planning a shotgun wedding. *His.* But she needed him with her, tomorrow at five. *God, please don't let this fall apart.*

"You're right."

Marianne blinked at him. "I am?"

Nick ran a hand through his impossibly mussed hair. "Totally right and, while I can't believe I'm saying this, we *are* engaged—*temporarily*. I need to step up, drive out to the Hamptons, and act the part. You're right. I'm sorry."

She nodded and bit down on her bottom lip. "Do you think we can pull it off?"

Nick smiled at her, and the temperature of the air around them seemed to warm. "Absolutely, and we kind of have to at this point, right?" He reached out to undo a couple of buttons at the top of the shirt she was wearing. "Besides, we've got the main thing down already."

"The main thing?"

"We've got chemistry." He bent his head to drop a soft kiss on her lips before letting his mouth cruise along her jawline, and she shivered in response. "See? We can sell the lie and nobody will be the wiser."

"But what if…"

"Marianne, you need to relax." He sank his hands into the hair at the base of her neck and let it fall through his fingers.

"What if I can't relax?"

"Then you need to stop talking."

Before she could respond, his lips covered hers, warm and gentle and heart-stoppingly sexy. A sigh parted her lips at the delicious sensation of his early morning stubble against her cheek. His tongue traced the line of her lips, so intimate and deep, and she tasted the bitterness of his morning coffee mixed with something else that was wonderfully masculine. God, she wanted to kiss him like this forever, not only for another thirty-six days. He pulled away slowly, lifting the collar of his shirt to frame her face before drawing her lips into one last kiss. Forehead pressed against hers, he said, "I'm hitting the shower."

Before he could get away she grabbed at the hem of his T-shirt. "Tell me what she said when you claimed to be my fiancé."

Nick slipped his shirt over his head. "I look forward to meeting you."

He walked toward the bathroom, and she padded after him. "That's all she said? I look forward to meeting you?" She stepped into the bathroom and caught Nick's image in the mirror.

And—wow.

Full frontal.

Her breath caught in her throat and all thoughts of expectations and plans hightailed it over to catch the jitney. How could she think about anything when Nick Wright stood in front of her totally naked? *Wow. Just wow.* Last night she'd tested her sexy flirtation steps and been rewarded with the best sex of her life and a night spent in his arms. Those incredible, unbelievable, sink-your-teeth-into-those-perfectly-sculpted-biceps arms. Nothing in her seduction hypothesis had prepared her for the male beauty standing in front of her. Michelangelo's David had nothing on the man. Her mouth went dry. She stared, her gaze raking over his lean, muscular body until she reached his midnight blues.

"I definitely cannot relax," she whispered.

He took a step toward her, a wicked grin creasing his impossibly gorgeous face. "Then you definitely need to stop talking."

Without warning, he scooped her into his arms and carried her into the shower. "Nick, what are you—put me down!"

The warm water from the showerhead fell against the bare skin of her thighs, drenching her wrinkled, slept-in shirt.

Nick wasted no time explaining his intentions. He pressed her body up against the cool tile of the shower as his mouth claimed hers in a soul shattering kiss. She clung to his shoulders as the water sluiced between them, running down her hair, her neck and shoulders, soaking his black cotton shirt. A moan escaped her as his mouth pulled away from her lips.

Dipping farther, his tongue ran across her collarbone, the heat of his kiss mixing with the water creating an effect so sensual and erotic, Marianne thought she'd die from the pleasure.

Nick turned his back to the water raining down on them, sheltering her from the direct blast. His hands slipped under the sides of her panties to cup her backside. She felt the solid muscle of his thighs, his erection against her hips. He pushed aside the wet collar of his shirt with his stubbled chin, and his mouth fell on her tightening nipples, warming them with his lips and tongue. Her eyes drifted shut behind her now steamy glasses, reveling in the feel of his mouth on her wet, naked breasts.

A small nip of his teeth sent a zing racing straight through her. God, simply kissing him made her body tremble and her heart soar, but seeing him this way, completely nude and wanting her: *more than she could imagine.*

"I know how to make you relax." God, that *voice.* His deep-toned, sexy words were enough to make her come right there without a single touch of his fingers.

His hands at her hips whirled her around until she pressed against the cool tiles. His hands slipped under the wet shirt, feeling her up from behind. The movement drew her closer, and she felt his erection press against her backside. Never in her wildest dreams had she imagined the mad rush of need unraveling inside her. She wanted to turn around and give him the erotic pleasure he showered down on her, but she didn't know what to do. She'd never wanted a man this way. Never knew it was possible to be so filled with desperate desire.

Marianne felt him smile against the nape of her neck as his fingers slipped inside her panties to find her damp. Her body moved against his playing fingers, eager to find release. His thumb circled, easing in and out of her in time with the seductive thrusts of his hips from behind. His mouth moved against her neck and jaw, tracing a hot, wet line to her earlobe as his hands continued their dual assault on her breasts and her clit. A whimper fell from her lips. If abandoning expectations meant feeling this sexy and wild, Marianne surrendered. She didn't want to be good, because being bad made her feel so damned incredible.

His fingers drifted away briefly, moving to her hips to flip her back around and press her into the corner of the tiled shower. His mouth moved to her lips, his nose bumping up against her glasses as he kissed her deeply and fully, in a way that exceeded even her most passionate dreams. She pulled off the horn-rims and shoved them blindly onto the nearby shelf. Her heart pounded against her chest as he dragged the wet panties down and slipped his fingers deeper inside, sending tiny bolts of lightning flashing through her.

"Come for me, Marianne."

Her whispered name on his lips sent her body into overdrive. Her breathing grew ragged, and she bit down hard on her bottom lip, whimpering softly, desperately close to climax. A pleading sound erupted from her throat as she felt the pleasure rush through her body, his strong fingers touching her, guiding her through a series of tremors fueled by raw, unmitigated desire. Her body spent, she curled against him, the water running down the shirt to caress her still-tingling skin.

"You are such a naughty girl." He pulled away just enough to look into her face, his wicked blue eyes shining through the water raining down around them. "So much I might have to be late for work."

"That naughty?" she whispered.

Nick dropped another slow kiss on her mouth before whispering against her parted lips. "Statistically speaking, much, much naughtier."

She smiled up at him, feeling the blush steal across her cheeks. "Is there another level of statistical naughtiness I might explore?" Her fingertips traced the line of hair that led down his abs to his throbbing erection. "Show me."

Nick let go a low curse, but took her hand and guided it to his rock-solid cock. A moan of pleasure ripped from his throat. She loved the feel of him in her hands, so hard and yet so vulnerable to her touch. He showed her how to coax his pleasure with her hand and she felt him harden further in her grasp.

"Oh, honey, yes." His deep, male groan echoed through the shower. "Yes."

She brought his mouth crashing down on her and kissed him with all the need he'd ignited inside her body and soul. Never had she felt so feminine and powerful. She'd moved way past siren. She was the exotic cake girl, and this morning she was not about to run away.

Instinctively she quickened the pace of her strokes until he went rigid in her hand, raw pleasure etched across his face as he came hard and fast.

Lost in the feel of him, she'd taken a wild chance and trusted him not to make her feel anything less than incredibly sexy. And he hadn't failed her. If anything, after this morning's shower, Marianne wanted to redefine sexy to include all kinds of hot new ideas. The best part was they still had five weeks left to experiment.

One hand on the tile behind her, Nick tilted forward to kiss her, and she returned his kiss wholeheartedly, turned on all over again by his charged reaction to their shower escapade. With his lips still a breath away, he wrapped his other arm around her waist, and together they slid to the floor of the shower, a tangled mess of limbs and wet clothes and spent desire.

The steam formed a heated cloud around them and he grinned over at her. "Definitely going to be late for work."

Chapter Twelve

"Develop a code to live by."
—mantelligence.com

Nick scrubbed his face with both hands. After wedging enough feminine gear into the trunk to wardrobe all of New York City's Fashion Week, he was more than ready to hit the road. "Marianne, please get in the car."

"That's a sports car." She eyed him over the rim of her sunglasses.

"No, Marianne, it's not just a sports car, it's a 1969 Alfa Romeo." Nick let go a sigh of frustration. She looked super-hot in those Hepburn-style Bans, but right now, super-hot was beside the point. Getting her ass in the car was the point.

"Do you know how much fuel that car uses? How many pollutants it disperses into the air?" She folded her arms across her chest in clear protest. "I can't go anywhere in that car."

He shrugged. "Well, then, you will be short one fiancé, because I am not driving out to the Hamptons in a freaking Prius." The fact that she looked completely adorable in a knee-length skirt, white T-shirt, and tennis shoes did not change his bottom line.

"My Prius gets the best EPA-rated gas mileage of any hybrid—over fifty miles per—"

"But how fast can she rev from zero to ninety?" He slid an arm around her waist and tugged her close, enjoying the feel of her in his arms.

She looked up at him, serious and sincere. "Environmentally sustainable materials are of much greater value than acceleration capabilities."

Nick smiled. His fiancée was a strictly by-the-speed-limit type of girl, a fact that only jacked up his seductive bent. Made him want to rock her world. He leaned close enough to whisper in her ear. "But how much fun is driving your Prius on the open road?"

Marianne swallowed hard and gave the sunglasses a quick stab with her index finger. "We had a deal."

"Yes, we did. I agreed to play fiancé for your family all weekend." Nick slammed the trunk shut, a clear indication that negotiations were over. "I did not agree to emasculate myself."

With a nod to the Alfa Romeo, she said, "That car is not your manhood."

"Maybe not, but it's damn close." He gave her a kiss hot enough to start his engine, and walked over to the passenger side and opened the door. "Please get in."

As he guided her into the front seat, she made a small sound in the back of her throat that reminded him of other sweet, sexy sounds. Maybe he'd pull off along the side of the road somewhere and school her in the benefits of a hot, sexy car.

He climbed in next and pressed a button on the console. The sleek black roof rumbled up and folded into the back of the car

"Hells bells, it's a convertible."

Nick smiled at her prim curse and revved up the engine. "Not just any convertible, honey, a 1969 Alfa Romeo Duetto Spider. Best ragtop in town."

"1969?" Marianne said, in an unexpectedly mischievous tone. "Think it'll make it?"

"Honey, this baby's got one hundred twelve horsepower, twin cam engine; it will not let you down." He pulled away from the curb. "And if you're really nice to me, I'll let you have your way with me in the backseat later."

She gave him a sidelong glance that promised all kinds of possibilities. "Keep driving."

Two hours later, as they approached East Hampton, the puzzle that was Marianne McBride started to come together. Or come apart, depending on your perspective. His fiancée was definitely coming unglued.

"Everything will be fine." Nick gripped the wheel and tried to play it cool.

Hell, a few days ago he lived by rules about back-to-back dates, and today he was playing *Meet the Parents*. One of them had to stay calm or this whole engagement fiasco was going to blow up like a bomb at the end of its timer.

"My parents never do anything small, so expect a lot of people—friends, neighbors—basically anyone who lives within a twelve mile radius," Marianne said, her voice so tense it sounded like she'd been hitting up a helium tank. "My dad's a sweetheart, but he's been through a lot, so try not to look directly at his ankle monitor," she continued at full speed. "Mom's an artist, and there's one of her paintings on every wall in the house. Compliment the artwork, but avoid any mention of Picasso, even his name…"

One hand on the wheel, he waved her words to a stop with the other. "Whoa, hang on just a minute. Your father's *ankle bracelet*?"

Marianne bit down on her bottom lip. "Yes…"

Nick drew in a breath and collected his thoughts. Minor offenses didn't normally require ankle monitors. "Start at the beginning."

In an obvious stall tactic, she adjusted her sunglasses against the bridge of her nose. "Until about a year ago, my dad owned a brokerage firm in Manhattan—upscale, extremely successful, high-profile clients."

Nick shifted in the leather seat, not liking where this story was going.

Hands clasped together and set primly on her lap, Marianne drew in a long breath and continued, "There was a rumor of securities fraud and my dad was arrested for insider trading."

Both hands white-knuckled the wheel. He was a financial attorney, for Christ's sake. A string of swear words bounced around in his head, Brooklyn-style curses, none of them nice, all more suited for a locker room than a trip to the Hamptons. He fought the urge to bang his palms against the steering wheel.

Marianne's brows pulled together. "Insider trading wasn't my dad's style. He worked by the book, but when the SEC filed charges, he refused to offer a defense and cut a deal, which still makes no sense to me." Looking away, she continued, "He did a six-month stint at a federal prison camp in Pensacola, minimum security, but … His firm still manages his investments, so it's not like he's banned from making profits, but the assets are monitored by the Feds."

"You should have told me." Her father's criminal history fell into the potential roadblock category where his career was concerned.

Marianne pulled her gaze from the road. "I'm sorry I didn't tell you. The party wasn't supposed to be for another two weeks, so I thought I'd have a chance, and given that our agreement was only for six weeks, I didn't think it was an issue."

"Well, it's an issue." Her card-counting secret paled in comparison to the unexpected news that her father had a permanent record. "Nothing I can't handle." But he wondered what else she kept hidden inside that proper exterior. "If he did his time, why the monitor?"

She bit down on her bottom lip. "Early release program, and now that he's out and his assets are partially unfrozen, my parents think it's time to celebrate."

Nick nodded, but kept his eyes on the road. "So this is why you're no longer a broker?"

An almost bitter laugh broke out of her. "Wall Street's a small world, so my dad's conviction cost me my career. Like father, like daughter rumors. None of them true, of course."

"Do you miss it? Wall Street, the action of the trading

floor?"

She gave him the sweetest, saddest smile, and a dull ache formed in the middle of his chest. Not at all straightforward or uncomplicated. "Do you know the only other person to ask me that is your sister? The only person in Manhattan who'd give me a chance. I owe her."

Nick nodded. "Explains the cake."

A blush colored her cheeks, but she waved away his remark, sexier in a ponytail than any woman who'd ever taken a ride in his backseat. Still, now that he'd discovered another of her secrets, he'd be smart to slow down. And not just his driving.

"To answer your first question—no, I don't miss trading. I still love numbers, their orderliness and dependability, but racking up dollars in my bank account was pretty empty."

She looked over, all clear blue eyes and windblown hair, and despite her secrets and her father's potentially career-damaging conviction, Nick felt something raw and primitive and protective release inside his gut, but he shoved the instinct aside. He needed to stay focused on his goals, his long-term, worked-his-ass-off-to-get-there goals.

"Oh, turn here." Marianne pointed toward an entrance half hidden by the tall sea grass and he made a hard left onto a pristine pebbled driveway. They drove a short distance along the shoreline to the water's edge where, surrounded by wide expanses of manicured lawn, stood an exquisite beach house. Strike that, a beach mansion.

"Holy shit." The hits just kept coming. He sure as hell wasn't in Brooklyn anymore.

Her fingers twisted the skirt's hem into a knot. "Six bedrooms, seven baths, every room with a view of Gardiner's

Bay."

"Even the bathrooms?"

"Even the bathrooms."

"Holy shit," he said again—for emphasis. *Definitely not Brooklyn.*

"Lord, here she comes." Marianne glanced up the driveway, exchanged the sunglasses for her spectacles, and straightened her shoulders as if expecting a hard line tackle from a Giants defensive back. Nick wondered why the hell she looked so uptight until…

"Oh, sweet baby chicken, you made it." A petite redhead waved at them, her heels crunching on the pebbled driveway as she approached. "Come here and give your mother a hug."

Rooted to the passenger seat, Marianne's eyes rounded at the words "sweet baby chicken," and her everyday blush turned raging scarlet.

"Mom, please, this is so not the time," she said, smoothing the line of her skirt.

Paying no attention, the woman pulled Marianne from the car and enveloped her into a bear hug that lasted a full two minutes. Finished, she gave the ring on Marianne's left hand a quick glance and trained her sights on Nick. "And this must be your new fiancé."

Nick plastered on his most charming smile and extended his hand. *Her* new *fiancé.* What the fuck. What the hell happened to her *old* fiancé?

"That's me," he said, with a pointed look at Marianne. "The new guy." His one and *only* fiancée was full of more secrets than Al Capone's vault.

"I like him," her mother said, accepting his hand with a sly smile. "A vintage Spider, a sapphire engagement ring, smart enough to propose to you—the man's a keeper."

A six week kind of keeper. He cocked an eyebrow, wondering how her family would react when fiancé number two hit the bricks.

Releasing his hand, Mrs. McBride linked her arm through her daughter's and started toward the house. "The barbecue starts at seven. Cocktails at six."

"But where's Dad?" Marianne asked, stumbling in her sneakers alongside her mom, her gaze searching back for Nick.

"With his parole officer."

Nick shot her a reassuring smile, pulled three suitcases from the back end of the car, and shut the trunk with a swift, solid crash. *Welcome to the Hamptons.*

A carnival.

Marianne stood under the twilight sky in the midst of a literal circus and sipped her vodka-laced frozen rainbow. While she wasn't much of a drinker, if there was a time to start drinking seriously, it was when your parents threw a welcome-home-from-prison carnival, complete with flamethrowers and funnel cake. If she could melt into the shimmering flagstone patio and leave her peep-toe heels behind, she would. Instead, she'd have to be content with retreating to the edge of the party until she could face down her ex, show off her sexy side, and make him eat his words. One by one. *But where was her impeccably charming date?*

She took a sip of the multicolored drink as her gaze scanned the crowd until she saw him—not Nick. Her ex, her proverbial nightmare, her *Jason* — and not like sexy-soap-opera-hero Jason, more like *Friday-the-13th*-mask-wearing Jason. Yes, that's who he was — her nightmare on Ocean Avenue. She wanted to stab him with her cocktail umbrella. He caught her eye and started toward her. She bit down hard on her bottom lip.

Where the heck was Nick?

In a moment of weakness, she considered bolting until she could find him, but blushing and bolting were the old Marianne's habits. While having Nick stand beside her all sexy and spectacular would have been ideal, he was…currently out of range. And while another two weeks of practicing her seductive skills would've been helpful, her dad's early release had made the additional practice impossible. But she was ready. She reached for her cardigan draped on the back of the wrought iron chair, but her fingers stopped short of picking it up. Cardigans were no longer required. She didn't need a cotton suit of armor. She needed confidence.

Marianne took another sip of her neon cocktail and shifted into her best Marilyn pose, shoulders back and down, one foot slightly in front of the other as if ready to step out and sashay. Despite the pose, a modicum of panic took residence in the back of her throat, but she refused to fall to pieces. If the cake jumping was her subway grate moment, then right now was *Some Like it Hot*, and she was ready to show her miserable cheating ex what he'd let go.

Jason worked his way across the lawn — without the dominatrix, she noted — and Marianne adjusted the sweetheart neckline of her light blue sundress to accentuate her sans-cardigan curves. Not flirting. Just underscoring her point.

Jason closed the last of the distance between them and, as the multicolored circus lights twinkled down from the palm trees, he leaned in and kissed her cheek.

An old reflex reared its ugly head, and she closed her eyes and breathed in his Dial soap and musk scent. But she felt nothing. A twinge of annoyance or irritation, maybe, a bit of curiosity about the missing dominatrix, but otherwise…nothing. Even the desire to stab him with the cocktail umbrella had evaporated into the night air. Certainly, there was none of the panting, desperate heat she felt when she looked at Nick. None of the longing that accompanied even his simplest kiss. With Nick, the world fell away.

Right now, Marianne knew exactly where she stood—across from a man who'd stolen a part of her. A part she hadn't known was missing until her time in close proximity to Nick. A part she was ready to reclaim.

"Hello, Marianne." Jason smiled, attractive in his polo-shirted, moneyed way. "You look…different."

"Different?" Not exactly the when-did-you-get-so-smoking-hot/I-was-a-fool-to-let-you-go reaction she'd been imagining, but she tried hard not to let him crawl under her skin.

"Different," he said, lowering his voice to the level of secrets. "And amazing."

"Thank you." Marianne offered a tight smile. The past ten months, all she'd wanted was to prove him wrong—prove she wasn't an ice queen—maybe hear him say she looked *amazing*. But now that he'd said it, she simply wanted to forget the past and move on. Even if he'd failed to be loyal to her, he'd been an invaluable asset to her father. "Thank you for helping my dad. I understand you worked to secure his early release."

He buried his free hand into the pocket of his Jack Spade Bermudas and eased back on his leather sandals. "The least I could do for my mentor, a man who was like a father-in-law to me."

Almost exactly like a father-in-law. The thought provided more relief than regret.

"Where is your new girlfriend?" Marianne asked, raising her hand to gossip behind the tips of her fingers in the way she'd seen people do, as if the existence of a dominatrix was too hush-hush to say aloud.

He raised his glass of white wine in a kind of mock good-bye. "No longer my girlfriend."

Funny, how she'd never noticed his white wine fixation before. Never red wine or tequila or dark beer, nothing to stain his designer clothes. "Decided she preferred a different kind of kinky?"

He raised his eyebrows in an expression filled with humor and surprise. "Listen to you, kitten. Less than a year away from the Street and you've got claws."

Marianne circled her vodka-based carnival-in-a-cup with the red and white striped straw. "Oh, I've learned a few tricks since you and your ex-dominatrix sent me packing. More than a few, actually." Her gaze searched the starlit patio for Nick and found him walking toward her, leaving behind her father and his parole officer, each one of them holding an extra-large cone of cotton candy. She glanced back at her ex. "And for the record, I never liked being called kitten."

A misty-eyed, almost pleading look ambled across his face, and he reached for her elbow, only to be edged out of the way by her bigger, brawnier fiancé.

"Hello, gorgeous," Nick said, dropping a lingering kiss on her mouth before handing over the sugar-spun candy. "Your dad's been showing me around the place."

Flushed and unreasonably pleased to see him, Marianne smiled up at him, lifted a couple inches of the pink confection from its cone, and settled a bit on her tongue. She let its sweetness melt in her mouth, and imagined licking the tasty treat from her fiancé's lips. Or other less accessible places. A warmth that had nothing to do with vodka stole through her system and she pulled more candy from the cone as her gaze drifted south along the line of Nick's body.

He looked so yummy wearing a sand-colored linen shirt, open at the collar, and a pair of navy pants that showed off his muscular hips and thighs to such perfection. She dragged her gaze back to his eyes to keep from staring. Wow, the thoughts he made race through her brain. She shook her head and raised another piece of the candy to her lips. *Delicious.*

Jason cleared his throat, and she blinked over at him, surprised again by how the world simply fell away whenever Nick was close enough to touch. Blushing, she turned back toward her ex and dropped a bombshell smile. "Jason, this is my fiancé, Nick Wright." She looked up at him from beneath her lashes. "Nick, Jason Ward."

MasterCard priceless. There was no other way to describe the look on her ex's face. No calculation or analysis could capture the way his smile faltered, the way the color drained from behind his spring tan. *The blond highlights. The sexy sundress. The updated eyewear with the perfect amount of bling.* All absolutely priceless when compared to the look of shock on her ex-fiancé's face.

Never a woman who enjoyed another person's discomfort, a twinge of guilt twisted in her stomach. But then she remembered her hopeful willingness, the satin panties, the dominatrix. *Timid. Hopeless. Ice queen.* She drew in a wobbly breath. Misplaced guilt would have to wait.

The men spent a minute sizing each other up before Nick extended his hand. "Jason."

"Nick." He reached out to accept the handshake, and she noticed how he seemed dwarfed by Nick's build and presence. "Engaged? Not expected, but congratulations seem to be in order."

Not expected. Marianne fought an urge to wrinkle her nose at the condescending comment. "And yet, current statistics show that four out of five people fall in love within one year of a breakup."

Jason gave her a flirtatious wink. "But do statistics show how long that kind of love lasts, Marianne? Or are you simply talking about a rebound relationship?"

Nick smiled easily, letting his fingers rest on her hipbone in a proprietary way that screamed, *back off, she's mine.* The caveman move sent a girly thrill racing up her spine and made her want to sneak into the clown's tent and shimmy out of her sundress.

"I don't know about you, Jason," he said in a low voice tinged with warning. "I'm not much of a statistics guy, unless we're talking quarterback ratings, and yet, I fell for this woman at first glance." He made a sexy sound of approval in the back of his throat. "One look at her curves in this hot, silvery dress, and I'll tell you, I was lost."

Lost.

Yes.

That's exactly how she'd felt.

He grinned down at her like a man in real love. She took a breath and reminded herself that their engagement was temporary, a six-week run that closed as soon as the show was over. Still, when he looked at her that way, convincing her heart of their short-term status proved to be difficult, especially when it all felt so real. "Funny how that can happen."

"Funny." His fingers fanned out, skimming her hips and upper thigh, and Marianne felt the temperature between them rise into the red zone. *Not timid or hopeless or icy.* Her gaze moved back to her former fiancé, and she was pleased to find him staring, practically open-mouthed—like a carp. She shifted toward him in that innocent, Marilyn way she'd practiced. "Some loves do last, Jason."

His gaze raked over her body, seeming to take in how Nick's palm had drifted south and now rested firmly across her backside. *Probably wondering if she let Nick spank her.*

"My loss," he said, pressing his hand to his chest in a mock gesture of pain. "But maybe we can put the past behind us. Get a drink next time I'm in the city."

Meeting up with Jason didn't interest her in the least, but she played along. "We'll have to check the calendar, right, honey?"

Nick nuzzled her cheek in an intimate gesture that was all kinds of possessive, and Marianne felt her breath catch in her throat. She was overheating like a late-night bonfire on Montauk Beach. "Why don't you call my office?" Nick said.

A small, hopeful smile touched her lips. Was she misreading the situation, or was Nick actually staking his claim? Could he be jealous?

Marianne shook away the notion. He'd agreed to play the charming fiancé, and he was simply doing a bang-up job. The annoyance written on his face at her subtle flirtation, at the mention of an off-the-books date with her ex was all in her imagination. Then he reached for her cardigan and draped it securely over her shoulders. *Definitely a caveman move.*

Marianne gave him a sidelong look and let the sweater fall away, but before she could blink, he was easing it back over her shoulders, buttoning the top button as if saying it was fine for him to encourage and embrace her wild, cake girl side. But as for anyone else…forget it. She turned her attention briefly back to her ex and said, "Yes, call the office and we'll see if we can make it happen."

Jason offered a slow nod of comprehension. "Call your office. Absolutely. Where are you working, Nick?"

Her fiancé's muscles tensed, but his easy smile never wavered. "Morgan Wealth Management & Trust. Midtown."

She smiled up at him. "Nick's about to make partner at the firm."

"Impressive," Jason said, his indifferent expression belying his words, "I'm considering a hedge fund investment. Maybe I throw some business your way?"

Marianne felt Nick turn to stone at her side. "Be my guest."

Another nod. "Nick Wright, Morgan Trust. I will definitely be in touch." Jason returned their smiles, but the way he spoke felt off, like it was part promise, part veiled threat. He lifted his drink in lieu of a handshake. "Enjoy the carnival."

As he walked away, Marianne's eyes narrowed on his back. Something about his cagey exchange with Nick made her decidedly ill-at-ease when she ought to be celebrating. She'd done it, convinced her ex-fiancé's cheating ass that she'd moved on with the world's most perfect man. A feat that seemed impossible a week ago. And she owed it all to Nick, her six-week fiancé. A small stab of pain twisted in her chest. Her time with Nick was already 17 percent over. She winced. Only 83 percent left.

"Everything okay?" Nick asked, his chin nestled against her temple, the tension seemingly melting away from his body.

"Everything is okay." Everything except how her heart would suffer when the percentages failed to work in her favor.

Marianne leaned her head back against his chest and gazed at the bright lights of the miniature Ferris wheel in the distance. There was only one man at this carnival she wanted to take for a spin tonight. The man who held her in his arms and made her feel protected and free. She turned around in his arms slowly, letting her breasts skim across his chest as her palms ran up his chest to the open neck of his shirt.

Her hands slipped inside his collar, and she took a step back, enjoying the heat of his gaze skimming over the curves of her body. She drew in a soft breath and unbuttoned the cardigan. The thin cotton fell away from her shoulders tugging the straps of her sundress down an inch or two on both sides. She tossed him a naughty smile. "Ready to take a ride?"

Nick glanced over his shoulder and quickly back. "Is that a trick question?"

Chapter Thirteen

"Listen more, talk less."
— mantelligence.com

"Don't move."

Sweet Jesus, Nick wasn't going anywhere. Not now. Maybe not *ever*.

Across the dimly lit third floor bedroom, Marianne eased the strap of her sundress away from her shoulder. Outside, the carnival rolled on, noisy and bright and crowded. But here in this intimate, quiet room, it was just the two of them, and Nick had never felt so turned on in his life.

Holding his gaze, Marianne bit down on her bottom lip as her hand moved to the side zipper. She tugged on the pull slowly and the sound of the small metal links unzipping echoed across the room. He made a move toward her, but she held up her palm. "Not yet," she whispered in a sweet, shaky voice.

Nick pressed his back against the door and stayed put, ready to do anything she asked. Marianne was in the driver's seat, and he was enjoying every single second of watching her move along the road to seduction.

In an achingly adorable motion, she eased the pastel blue fabric down one arm and then the other until she was naked from the waist up. No striptease had ever been this sweet. Or this hot. His palms itched to touch her. He wanted to breathe her sweet, citrus scent, taste the salt air on her skin.

She was beautiful.

Crazy-beautiful.

He'd seen a lot of attractive women, but not one of them struck a chord in him like his fiancée. She was too good for him, so smart and freaking sexy, but awkward and vulnerable, too, an intoxicating mix. Maybe it was his protective instincts kicking in, but staying away from her was becoming impossible. He'd actually been jealous of her ex, the way he'd looked at her like he'd known her. Nick knew better. If he'd really known Marianne, he never would have let her go.

She wriggled the dress away from her hips and let the fabric fall to the floor in a blue pool at her feet. Naked. His sexy-sweet cake girl stood before him naked. He'd been expecting a glimpse of lacy panty, but his woman had stepped it up a notch, and he was freaking speechless. He wanted to move. He wanted to wrap her up in his arms and kiss her but remained rooted to the spot, his back pressed hard against the back of the door.

Jesus, she was perfect. He'd already touched her, enjoyed every inch of her body, but to see her trembling and naked, gorgeous and wanting, Nick felt as if he couldn't breathe.

Her flushed skin glowed in the dim lamplight, and a shadow fell across the delicate collarbone that framed her lush breasts. Rosy nipples beaded in the night air, begging to be warmed by his tongue. Her waist and hips curved in a bombshell figure straight from an old-time movie, and he wanted to grab on and plunge into her depths as she wrapped those killer legs around him. Oh yeah, they were going on a ride tonight, a long, sexy ride that would make her cry out in desperate pleasure.

She crooked a finger at him, and he had to fight the urge not to run across the room.

Nick walked toward her in an even stride that left no room for objection. He took her face in his hands and kissed her. Slowly. Deeply. Then he fell to his knees at her feet. She stepped out of her dress and he moved to slip off her sexy, open-toed shoes, but her whispered words stopped him mid-motion.

"Leave them on."

Sweet mother of God.

That hot command falling from her sweet lips was more than he could take. He gazed up at her as his palms skimmed the back of her calves and her thighs, gliding over her silky skin to cup her gorgeous ass. He stood and dragged her body against his. He wanted to be gentle, to take it slow, but he was damned if he could control his response to her adorable little striptease. This woman was driving him crazy. Hot. Did. Not. Begin. To. Cover. It. Nick was on fire for her.

He wanted her. All of her and he wanted her now. Off-limits had skipped town days ago. And in this moment, he didn't care about potential career pitfalls or secrets.

He bent his head and captured her lips with his, kissing

her, nipping at the fullness of her bottom lip, tasting the sweetness of her, reveling in her innocent temptation. His hands caressed the line of her naked back as his mouth ravaged her lips. There was something so naughty and erotic about her standing there, with nothing on but her sexy shoes, while his mouth roamed her skin. But he wanted more.

As if sensing his need, her hands fumbled with the buttons on his shirt. But he couldn't wait another second. He needed her now.

"Tear the damn thing open," he said in a low, desperate voice he almost failed to recognize as his own.

She gave him no reason to ask twice as her fingers tore at the buttons and ripped open the shirt in one swift move. Small hands pressed the fabric away from his shoulders and down his back. The linen hit the floor. Her body arched toward him, easing up against his half-naked body, and a soft sigh fell from her lips. Her eyes darkened as her gaze raked over him, filled with a wonder and need that sent his blood pressure skyrocketing. With his fingers buried in the golden hair at her nape, he kissed her temples and her jaw and her lips. Her palms slid across his shoulders and down his chest. He pressed a little closer, his need to feel her beneath him growing intense. In answer, her fingertips burned a trail along his ribcage, moving low across his abs before moving to the waistband of his pants.

She undid the button and lowered the zipper with a soft sigh. Something about her wild, pleading moans and her agonizing sighs spoke straight to the man in him. A secret smile crossed her pretty face as she dragged the soft cotton pants over his ass and down his thighs, letting her fingers skim along his muscles in a not-so-innocent game of seduction. He kicked off his leather shoes, hustled his pants from his ankles, and looked down at her. She was on the floor on her knees, and the sight of her gazing up at him, her blue eyes filled with longing, sent him reeling

His body shook as she ran her tongue along his erection, hardening him further—a feat he hadn't thought possible— as she took him into her mouth. God, he'd never known he could feel so powerless at a woman's touch. He bore her ministrations for as long as he could, savoring every caress of her mouth and hands on his cock, then he reached for her and dragged her up his body. No more teasing. No more aching touches. Tonight he planned to bury himself deep within her, starting right freaking now.

"Marianne," he said in a husky voice, "I plan to show you how sexy you are, prove how much you turn me on, and when I'm finished, you are going to cry out my name in absolute need. Can you promise me that? Because I want to hear you say my name when you come. Promise me."

"I promise," she whispered.

He nodded. "Make good on that promise, Marianne, and we'll do it again."

She ran her tongue over her lips and reached back for the condom she'd left on the nightstand. "We will?"

Nick lifted her into his arms, his hands cupping her ass. "Oh honey, we will. Because I promise you…I can last all night long."

Cradling her against him, he bent his lips to kiss her, enjoying the cotton candy and vodka mix, letting his tongue intertwine with hers, as they fell back against the bed in a hot, playful tangle. Nick reached for her hips and she straddled him, her take-me-now shoes dangling off the edge of the bed.

"You are beautiful."

She bit down on her bottom lip and looked away, but he couldn't let her doubt for a moment that she was spectacular. His palms ran along the hourglass curve of her waist to the side swells of her breasts. "Marianne, look at me." Her gaze slid back to him. "Beautiful."

He raised his lips to her right breast and took her rosy nipple into his mouth, tasting her skin, sucking on her flesh until her body arched and bucked against him. He could feel her wet, slick core against his skin. She felt so good, he wanted to plunge inside her and make her cry out his name, but he wanted more. He wanted her to feel desperate and hungry for him. He wanted her to know what it felt like to feel utterly desired. To feel bewitched. Because that was how he felt.

Nick eased back and let her restless body move against him. He murmured his encouragement, letting his thumbs graze the tips of her breasts. God, he loved seeing her this way, vulnerable to his heated touch, responding to his every caress. Her eyes drifted shut, and he continued to stroke and tease until she threw back her head and let go a husky whimper. He grabbed hold of her hips.

Another moan escaped her lips. Her body grew more impatient, and he ached to fill her, to drive home the depth of his need for her. He raised her hips, positioning her heat above his throbbing erection. She ripped open the condom with her teeth and slid it on him before slowly lowering her hips, taking him inside her inch by inch. He rocked her gently, increasing the rhythm as her breath grew ragged. Hands on her hips, he coaxed her closer, driving upward as she slammed against him searching for a climax. She ran her hands up her ribcage to cup her breasts. His dick responded to the sight of her touching herself, holding and tweaking her nipples to bring her closer. Fuck. He drove her harder.

"That's right, honey, show me," he groaned. "Show me what you want."

"I want you, Nick." She cupped both her breasts in her hands and gazed down at him. "I want you."

She bucked against him, her legs wrapped around him, the click of the high heels meeting with each thrust. The sound drove him wild. He ran his free hand down the length of her legs, following the trail back upward to gently knead her ass, desperate to be closer to the heart of her.

"Marianne, you feel so good. I want to hear you come for me."

She threw her head back, crying out as she reached a shattering orgasm. "Oh God, Nick, I'm coming, I'm coming."

He felt the waves of pleasure crash through her body and he pressed his lips to hers. Softly. Gratefully.

He took in the quiet beauty of her flushed face, lost in the pleasure of her blue eyes, the hush of her shallow breathing, the slight tremble of her bottom lip. The feeling of being surrounded by this gentle, tender woman was so exquisite he couldn't bear for it to end. Not yet. Maybe not ever. His hands found her face, his fingers sinking into her silky hair. Breathing in the provocative scent of her skin, he eased all the way out of her until they were still barely connected and thrust back inside slowly. Once. Twice. His gaze measured her response as her body rose to meet each of his deliberate, unhurried strokes. Her lips parted in an invitation he could not turn down, and he kissed her, caressing her with his tongue, intensifying the spark of desire reigniting between them. Slow and steady, he built her up again.

"Oh please," she begged, her eyes wild.

And the sounds she made…*damn*. He felt the tension ramp up inside her body. Felt her reach for him. Felt her need. He slammed against her, his body shaking, holding firm and fast, waiting for her next release. He moved faster, his fingers curled into her hair, his gaze locked onto her face as she shattered into a thousand beautiful pieces.

"Oh, God, Nick, I'm coming," she cried out.

Damn, he loved his name on her lips. He rode her through it, then eased back, waiting—praying—she could come apart in his arms yet again.

It was a while before her breathing slowed. When she finally came back to herself, she touched his face. "I didn't know it could be like this."

Yeah. Neither did he.

Oh, he was good. But this insane need to feel her body rise and demand and tremble, it was insatiable. Primal. The hottest fucking thing he'd ever experienced.

He kissed her softly, reverently, and began to thrust deep inside her. He wanted to hear her cry out his name again and again, until she understood that she belonged to him. And when her arms came around him, tugging him to her, chest to chest, heart to heart, her lips pressed to his throat in a sweet, desperate kiss, he finally followed her over the edge.

A soft ocean breeze drifted in from the open window. Cool. Sweet. Sounds of the carnival filtered in from far away, but there was nowhere else in the world Nick would rather be than here, right now, in this moment of pure sensual satisfaction. Marianne curled against him, her body supple and warm. His fingers skimmed her hip as she gazed up at him. "So…that was kind of incredible," she said, her glasses all off-kilter.

He smiled and pulled the frames away from her face so he could look at her. She was so crazy-beautiful. And there definitely *was* something about the glasses—the process of stripping them away, revealing her sweet blue eyes, as clear and intoxicating as a summer sky.

He twisted around and set her glasses on the nightstand and turned back to kiss her again. "Damned incredible if you ask me."

Marianne looked up at him through her lashes. "Only another twelve hours or so before we have to pack up your environmentally challenged car and drive back to Manhattan."

"Only twelve hours? What should we do with twelve hours?"

"Well…we could sleep…" She ran a peep-toe heel along the inside of his calf. "Unless you have a better idea."

"Honey, I have all kinds of *better ideas*." Nick reached out and pulled her on top of him, all hard and ready for another chance to live out his cake girl fantasy. "No sleep required."

Chapter Fourteen

"Whatever happened, don't let your fear of the past control
your plans for the future."
—mantelligence.com

Every minute of the weekend with Marianne was fantastic, but now Nick was back at work with a shitload of issues to deal with and a few worries about John McBride's legal issues potentially blowing up in his face. Worries he placed at the feet of his little sister.

"Jesus, Jane, don't you get it? I'm an attorney." He punched up the volume on his cell and walked to the far side of his office with half a mind to strangle her. Slowly. With his bare hands. "You are the matchmaker who set me up with a woman who is potential career kryptonite." And he was too deep in the relationship to back out now.

He thrust his free hand into his hair and tried to stay calm. While it was true his sister had set him up with his temporary fiancée, if he was honest, the shitstorm he was in now was entirely his fault. He was the guy who'd promised his boss he could deliver the perfect fiancée. He was the guy who'd been arrogant enough to fall into a relationship with his sister's off-limits friend, and then cross way over the off-limits line.

"Nick, you're not a criminal attorney, you're a finance guy." His sister's impatient sigh echoed through the fiber optics.

"Yes, that's right." Frustration tightened his jaw and paced across his office, practically wearing a groove in the corporate industrial carpet. "A financial *attorney* who deals with a truckload of private equity, and my fiancée's father is a felon convicted of insider trading."

"A small white-collar crime."

Like a white-collar crime amounted to nothing. Jesus, reputation was everything in his business. He lowered his voice and cupped the cell in his hand. "Not a small deal over at Morgan Wealth & Trust. Much closer to money laundering than a bank error."

Goddammit. He balled his hand into a fist and strode over to the window, looking for something to hit. He was far from perfect. Hell, it's not like he hadn't boosted a lawn chair or two or scammed pizza slices out the back door of Salvatore's back in Brooklyn, but insider trading was no kid's misdemeanor. If the firm caught wind of the fact that he was marrying into a family with a felony conviction, his partnership bid would evaporate in a cloud of legal smoke. Not that he was really marrying Marianne, but hell…she'd made him actually consider that his work-centric life was empty. She made him feel…damn, all the clichés…she made him feel *complete*. God, just having that thought made him want to punch something.

But was he really willing to blow his dream job and everything he'd worked for? And if he did take a stab at a relationship that lasted longer than a weekend, would he be capable of honoring a commitment? He'd seen his father gamble and drink himself out of his marriage. Why the hell did he think he'd be any different? Sure, he'd always tried to be, but…

"Nick? Are you there?" His sister's voice interrupted his internal tirade. "I'm sorry. I didn't know this would create a problem for you, and yes, okay, maybe I should have thought it through more, but…"

Nick ran a hand along his jaw, his patience wearing way past thin. "Maybe?"

"But I *know* you. I know what will make you happy."

"Can you please cut me some slack here, Cupid?" Since becoming engaged, his sister saw love-despite-all-obstacles on every street corner. She was driving him insane. "Your latest matchmaking stunt could cost me my damned career." Jane started to protest, but a knock on his door demanded his attention. "Don't bother to deny it. I know everything. I gotta go. I'll call you later."

"Promise?"

Nick sighed. No matter how crazy she made him, Jane was his little sister, the one he'd managed to put through college and keep out of serious trouble. Yeah, no matter how much trouble she caused or havoc she wreaked, he'd always be there for her. "Promise." He ended the call and looked over at his boss.

"Nick, sorry to interrupt, but I wanted to let you know

I'm about to meet with the board about your partnership. Given the way everything is shaping up, my guess is you're a shoo-in. Another week or two and your name will be embossed on the letterhead." Dan walked into the office extended his hand. "I'm proud of you, kid. You deserve it."

"Thanks, Dan." A not-so-small measure of guilt bled into his pleasure at finally nailing down the partnership he'd worked so hard to win. Yes, he'd earned it through hard work and a successful run of legal and investment advice for his clients, but his fake engagement—his lie—had been the thing to push him over the goal line. A fact that merited no celebration.

"Can't happen fast enough, either. I got a call from a new client this morning requesting you manage his portfolio. I need you to get to work on it right away, so we can secure his business." Dan tapped through the confidential screen on his tablet. "Transferring the data now," he said, striding to the door. "And Nick?"

"Yes?" Nick verified receipt of the financials and looked over at his boss.

"Between now and your confirmation, can you do me a favor?"

"Absolutely."

Dan gave him a meaningful look. "Try not to screw up."

Nick waved his phone in response as a tight smile formed on his face while he watched his boss stride away. He was tired of everyone expecting the worst of him and often being right. The time had come to get his shit together and grow up. He wasn't just some Brooklyn scholarship kid hustling a good job, lucky to be at the party. He was a partner at Morgan Wealth Management & Trust. He'd made it. Or at least, he was a confirmation away.

And he owed it all to Marianne.

With his partnership practically secured, he'd be engaged another four or five weeks, after which he'd be a free man again. Ironically, and despite its nuclear potential, her father's conviction offered him an ironclad reason to break off the engagement, a perfect alibi. But he'd never use it. Their breakup would be quiet and painless. If he steered clear of complications for the next few weeks, he'd have everything he'd ever wanted.

So why did he feel so restless?

Nick grabbed the tablet, settled behind his desk, and punched in the codes required to open the transferred portfolio. As the financials filled the screen, Nick's jaw tightened. *Son of a bitch.* This. Was. Not. Happening. Nick pushed the tablet aside and tore both hands through his hair. His breakthrough client, the one who'd gone to such great lengths this morning to request him personally, belonged to none other than his fiancée's ex. *So much for avoiding complications.*

What? Did the asshat really think they'd be friends? That he'd actually pencil them in for drinks? He'd sooner tweezer his balls. Jason Ward was an asshole of epic proportions. The root, he suspected, of Marianne's insecurities. Hampton Boy had another thing coming if he thought for one second that Nick would clap him on the back and welcome his business with an IPA and a secret boys' club handshake. *Asshat.*

Some of his reaction came from feeling protective of Marianne. He could admit that, separate some of the emotional component. But of all the firms in the city, why would Jason Ward select his, and him specifically, unless he had some ulterior motive?

For a minute, Nick considered calling it a conflict of interest—after all, they'd both been engaged to the same woman—but forwarding his file could raise a red flag or two. *Never a good sign.* But he sure as hell didn't want to manage a deal for this guy. He was a snake, and Nick only dealt with people he trusted. Still he didn't want to rock the boat, not now, not with his confirmation so close. He tapped on the desk. What angle was this guy playing?

Over the next several hours, Nick worked his way through the restricted access screens, checking the basics, delving deeper into the timing of a few lucrative trades in speculative securities. Nick wasn't a criminal attorney, but from the looks of the files, he believed, Marianne's ex had been the dirty trader in her father's company. Now he wanted to move the profits into a hedge fund without drawing unwanted attention to his high-flying scores. And so he chose...Nick.

His fist hit the desk. *Enjoy the carnival, my ass.* The guy figured he'd play him. *Nick Wright, Morgan Trust. I will definitely be in touch.* Probably thought that with the engagement, Nick would be inclined to keep everything hush-hush, go along for the sake of male solidarity, take the money and run. Or maybe he figured the potential blow to Nick's career would force him to dump Marianne, and he'd ride in to save her like some kind of white knight in fucking Bermudas. Oh yeah. With startling clarity, Nick dialed in on the dickhead's intentions.

Too bad for the asshole that he'd failed to recognize Nick wasn't some Hamptons-style player inclined to look the other way. Nick was a Brooklyn guy with an instinct for secrets and an inability to hang a friend out to dry.

But what the hell was Nick supposed to do with his suspicions? The financials revealed some well-timed spikes in profitability, but no concrete proof, no evidence. He'd come to the firm to buy into a fund. Nothing shady about that deal. If Nick revealed his reservations, it wouldn't change the fact of John McBride's incarceration. Ward was a client now, so the ethics of such a revelation were dicey. Not to mention that those ethics would sure as shit cost him the partnership. *Dammit*. He'd thought if he played his cards right, kept a low profile, there'd be no reason for his fiancée's past to come back and bite him in the ass.

Obviously, he'd thought wrong.

Nick rose from his chair, strode over to the windows, and stared over at Brooklyn. He'd worked hard for a shot at having his name on the letterhead, but being with Marianne had made his work-centric life feel empty. The partnership issue wouldn't even be on the table without her. But was he willing to blow his dream job and everything he struggled to build? For her? For her family? He ran a hand along his jawline. And if he was, could he honor that kind of commitment? Or was he just like his father, good for the short-term until it was time to run?

His mind raced ahead of him, full of questions without answers. He walked back to the desk, and his gaze sharpened on the screen. Damn, he hated puzzles.

But in that moment, two things hit him as powerfully as a combination of jabs: One, Nick was not his father. And, two, he knew what he needed to do.

Marianne walked past Radio City Music Hall with a grin on her face. Maybe it was the springtime, but her heart felt hopeful about the future. A future with Nick. Could she dare to hope for that much? She imagined afternoons in Central Park and summers at the beach, taking him to the holiday show come winter, ice skating at Rockefeller Center. Touristy stuff, hokey to some New Yorkers, but she loved Christmas in the city. Sharing that time with Nick would be a dream come true.

While their engagement was still temporary, Marianne believed there was a chance they'd last beyond the six weeks. Despite all the statistics of failed relationships, she wanted a passionate love, full of sexy times in the shower and nights of lovemaking that led to a blissful nine hours of sleep in the arms of her man. She wanted a marriage, a real marriage, and had decided to tell Nick she wanted to take "temporary" off the table.

Counselor, she practiced in a husky, internal whisper. *I'd like to renegotiate our terms.*

She understood there would be no guarantees, no promises, but she'd done a cost-benefit analysis of the situation and made her decision. Nick might not be ready. Might never be ready. But she needed to find out. Because, despite his rules and serial dating ways, Marianne believed the matrix was correct. Nick was her perfect match. Deep in her soul, she felt Nick believed it, too.

A breeze kicked up the hem of her white silk skirt as she crossed over Sixth Avenue toward his office, and she let the material float above her knees. Spring filled the air, a picnic basket swung from the crook of her elbow, and she was on the way to offer her fiancé an office quickie. No more playing only the good girl.

The weekend in the Hamptons proved to be a revelation. She'd spent her life exceeding expectations, but the expectations were hers, not her parents. She'd always assumed the life her parents wanted for her. Made judgments about them. She'd never known her mom and dad married in a shotgun wedding complete with a midnight exit down a fire escape and the disapproval of her family. Marianne wanted more than the standard, probable outcome, too. She wanted Nick.

Marianne spun through the revolving glass doors of the Morgan building and practically into the arms of a man she recognized from the firm's casino night.

He reached out to steady her. "Marianne, right?"

She blinked twice and resettled the horn-rims against her nose. "Yes, I'm—"

"Going to see your fiancé," he said. "I'm Drew Evans. I work with Nick." He ushered her away from the door and glanced down at the basket swinging from her elbow. "Lunch, huh? Lucky guy."

She tightened her grip on the basket. Drew Evans might be smiling at her, but he didn't seem friendly. He seemed more like a man with an agenda. "I'm the lucky one."

"Seems like it," Evans tilted forward and lowered his voice, "considering how Nick pulled you out of thin air."

Her brows knit together. "I don't under—"

"No need to play games, Ms. McBride." He looked over his shoulder and then back to her, keeping his voice quiet. "That was quite a show you put on the other night."

"A show?" Unfortunately, his agenda was becoming as clear as the sky outside.

"Pretty good at cards for such a casual player. Made

me think you might be good with numbers, so I did a bit of research." He crossed his arms in front of his chest. "I think we both know *good with numbers* is an understatement."

Her uptown girl training kicked in, and she gave him a beatific smile that failed to reach her eyes, but telegraphed her cool disapproval to perfection. "Nice to have met you, Mr. Evans," she said, making a move toward the elevator, needing to tell Nick, to warn him.

"Not so fast, Marianne." Evans took a small step to block her path. "I know all about you and your not-so-squeaky-clean past."

Marianne's heart lodged in her throat. This could not be happening. She'd been avoiding the idea that her father's conviction could touch Nick. After all, she wasn't a trader anymore. Besides which, their engagement was only tempo-rary. But now she saw it was naive to think she could avoid a guy like Evans, even for six weeks.

His gaze took in her discomfort, and he smiled. "I've heard all the accusations that you were a dirty trader like your jailbird father, a garden-variety criminal all wrapped up in an angelic, buttoned-up package. But you're not so buttoned-up, are you?" He took a step back and straight-ened his tie, a mocking gleam in his eye. "I know you're smarter than to think your dad's conviction won't kill the Nickster's partnership dream. Once the board hears about daddy's indiscretions…well, let's just say, they are pretty conservative around here."

Her entire body trembled in anger. "Go to hell."

"Tough words from such a nice girl." He lifted the top of the basket, peeked inside, and let the wooden lid drop down with a soft whack. "Enjoy your lunch."

She watched him walk away. His words stung, but the truth of what he said hit home. Determined not to hurt Nick or be the cause of his partnership circling the drain, she decided to forget the steamy picnic. Instead of warning Nick, she'd go back to his apartment and clear out now before his colleague destroyed Nick's dream of a partnership.

Her heart might be broken, but his would survive. Let Nick tell the firm that she'd withheld the information, which, if she was honest with herself, in a way she had. Let him say he'd broken it off because of her deceit, that he was reeling from the end of his engagement, ready to devote all his resources to the firm.

Or maybe Jane could find him a second temporary fiancée who didn't have an unremitting scandal chasing her, one who could offer a long-term relationship, and a chance for a real love. The thought of Nick falling for another woman caused hot tears to form in the back of her eyes. But he deserved love. Even if he didn't know it, Nick was a man capable of real, true love, the kind Marianne finally understood. Hiking the picnic basket against her elbow, she walked back through the revolving doors to catch a cab back to SoHo, determined to pack up her six-week fantasy.

Her inner siren had gotten more than she'd bargained for when she'd popped out of that three-tiered cake. She'd been looking for a chance to bust out of her shell—to test drive her inner sex goddess and challenge her statistics and by-the-book ways. But Marianne McBride, part numbers girl, part seductress, had gotten so much more. Despite her intentions and plans, she'd fallen inescapably, irrevocably in love with her temporary fiancé. *Temporary*.

The word broke her heart.

Chapter Fifteen

"You might think that figuring them out is impossible, but don't worry; contrary to how it might seem, it's actually quite simple."
—mantelligence.com

Nick stood on the cobblestone sidewalk outside his building holding a bouquet of daisies. A set of storm clouds created shadows in the evening sky, forecasting the rain that was sure to come. Perfect weather for his mood. He looked up at his darkened condo and reached up to undo his tie. He'd expected Marianne to be home, but maybe she was in the back and had turned off the lights she wasn't using, conservation being one of her causes. He walked into the building, gave a short wave to Max who looked as anxious as Nick had ever seen him. Normally, he'd stop and talk Yankees baseball with the guy, but tonight Nick headed straight to the elevator, needing to hash everything out with

Marianne.

He'd suffered through a long-ass day, but in the end, he'd decided to tell her his suspicions about Jason Ward. He hoped she didn't still harbor any feelings for the guy. Personally, he wanted to string him up by his nuts and hang him from a tree branch in Central Park for what he'd done to Marianne and to her family. But his fiancée was a better person than him. If anything, she'd want to take the blame for not catching Ward's con. But she was trusting, and even the smartest people can be taken in by trusting the wrong kind of love.

He stepped out of the elevator and walked down the hall.

The thought of telling Marianne turned his stomach. He hated the idea that she'd feel responsible for her father's conviction. He'd even picked up daisies from a street vendor, hoping the flowers would soften the blow, which was ridiculous considering the news. But if he was right, and he was certain he was, the time had arrived to lay all the cards on the table and get to the truth. Even if the truth cost him his job.

Together, he and Marianne would work to prove her father may have been guilty of a quick sell-off, but that he was also railroaded by a man he trusted like a son. After that, maybe they'd find a criminal attorney to work toward a reversal. He shook his head, not having thought that far. He simply needed to be truthful with her. No secrets. No cons.

He swiped his key and walked inside the condo. His instinct was to call out to her, but a sinking feeling in his stomach quieted the words on his lips. No music. No humming. No welcoming orange-blossom scent. The sinking feeling turned to stone in his gut.

"Marianne?" *Where the hell was she?* If she'd stayed late at Cupid or gone out to dinner with Jane, she would have called or sent a text. He looked at his phone. No messages.

Concerned now, he strode deeper into the condo—not in the kitchen, or the living room. Then he checked the bedroom, and her perfectly starched skirts were gone. A quick glance in the bathroom confirmed her overly floral hair and skin products had vanished, too. She couldn't have simply left. Or could she? Maybe she'd gotten what she needed from their six-week deal and decided to call it quits. No, she wasn't the kind to grab and go. He shook his head and returned to the main living area, stopping short of the black marble island in the kitchen. Shimmering on the center of the marble was his mother's sapphire ring, no note, no box, no nothing.

He felt a kick of bitterness in his gut. Could he really have been that wrong about her? Had she really used him as protection against her ex only to renege on the rest of the deal? His jaw tensed. One thing was sure, he intended to find out. He called her cell. No answer. He considered calling Jane, but no, this was between him and his fiancée. He stormed to the door. He planned on finding her and getting the truth. Even if it meant knocking on every upscale door in Gramercy Park.

"No games, Marianne, let me in. I need to talk to you." On the other side of her door, Marianne bit down on her bottom lip and debated her next move. Part of her wanted to see Nick more than anything in the world, but another part of her knew that if she looked into his eyes or got caught up in his smile, she'd confess the truth about his colleague's threats, and the thought of what he'd do with that information sent a shiver of concern down her spine.

"Now is not a good time, Nick," she said, wincing at the string of curse words he muttered in response.

When he spoke again his voice was low and controlled. "It's raining, and you owe me an explanation. Let me in, please." He didn't ask again, and the silence stretched on, punctuated by the banging of her heart. She drew in a shaky breath and wiped her damp palms on the front of her denim coveralls.

He was right. She owed him an explanation. And making him stand out there in the rain was not acceptable. She put down the pry bar and the hammer, unlocked the deadbolts and opened the double-sided wooden doors. Nick stood on the stone steps beneath an old-fashioned light fixture, dressed in his suit, his tie loose, a bouquet of beat-up daisies in his hand. His hair damp from the rain, he looked tired and gorgeous and guarded.

Her heart ached at the sight of him. "How did you find the right house?"

"That's all you've got? How did you find the right *house*?" He shook his head and answered. "I'd intended to knock on every door in your exclusive neighborhood, even jump the damned fence if necessary, but disturbing the peace didn't seem like such a great idea, so I called my sister from the taxi. She gave me your address." He ran a hand through his damp hair. "Today's been a shit day. Didn't want to add getting thrown in the clink to the list." His jaw tightened as if it took all his control not to drag her out and demand answers. "Sorry, that was insensitive."

She wanted to kiss away the tension on his face. Instead, she stabbed at her glasses with her index finger. "That's okay."

The light from the porch created shadows beneath his eyes, but his tone was unnervingly calm. "It's raining. May I please come inside?"

"Yes, of course. I'm sorry." Marianne stepped back and waved him inside, feeling as awkward as she had outside her gym a week ago. *One wonderful whirlwind week.*

She shut the door and turned around. Nick stood in the middle of the brownstone, his expression registering the sheet-covered furniture, dusty floors, and old farm-style cabinets lined up on the drop cloth next to the kitchen. He looked big and powerful and sexy. Her eyes closed against the fantasies running through her mind. Fantasies of Nick making love to her in her tiny bedroom in the back, filling the place inside her body that needed him, craved him like she'd never craved any other man. A rush of heat suffused her body from deep inside, and she knew it would take every ounce of strength to turn him away.

His gaze moved over her from her dust-specked glasses to yellow tank top and oversized coveralls all the way down to her sneakered feet. "Renovating started already?"

She nodded, unable to speak past the lump in her throat.

"See, that doesn't add up to me." He took a step toward her and the razor-sharp movement changed the relaxed, cool version of Nick into an edgy-looking, slightly dangerous version, despite the sweet daisies he gripped in his hand. "Why start renovations if you intended to break our agreement?"

"I never intended…" Marianne shut her mouth on the rest of the explanation. Revealing the truth meant revealing his colleague's threats, and she needed to let him believe she simply wanted out. A difficult choice, but she never should have exposed him to the issue of her father's conviction in the first place.

"You can't just pack up and walk out. We have an agreement, and, honey, I have more than fulfilled my side of the bargain."

More than fulfilled. Maybe it took the scandal and quitting her job for her to reevaluate her life. But it took Nick to start her living it. She'd been keeping up some self-imposed standard for her parents, and then for her fiancé, and it wasn't until those two standards were destroyed that she started to ask herself, *What do I want?* Maybe seeing the devotion and love between her parents and how much they stuck together through the ups and downs showed her that money and labels didn't mean much without love. But it was Nick who made her believe in love. Even better, he made her realize she deserved it.

Marianne looked at him through the tears stinging her eyes.

He took a step closer. "Are you reneging on the engagement? Because it sure as hell feels like you've been using me to get some kind of twisted revenge on your ex, and now that you've got it, you decided to take off."

Letting him believe that broke her heart to pieces, but it had to be done. Her whole body trembled in preparation of her words. A six-week engagement had seemed like a perfect solution to both their problems, but Evans was right about one thing. She was smart enough to know better, and now she needed to protect her fiancé.

She drew in a shaky breath. "It was a mistake. The engagement…the lies…everything. All a mistake."

"Is this about your father's conviction? About how his conviction might affect my partnership?" he asked, his keen mind right on the money, as always.

She shook her head. "No, why would any of that matter to—"

"Because I don't give a shit about my reputation or the damn job. All I want is you."

The words echoed through her torn-apart townhouse, everything she wanted to hear—and he might even mean it now. But he wouldn't always. He'd regret his words one day, and Marianne refused to be the cause of his regret. When the time arrived, and he looked at her and wished he'd made a different choice, it would kill her. "Nick, I think you need to leave."

A muscle ticked in his jaw. "According to our agreement, you owe me six weeks. I've got five more, and you are coming home with me tonight."

Home. More than anything she wanted to go home with Nick. She wanted to sneak up onto the rooftop and make love with him under the stars and forget how her choice to jump out of his birthday cake and into his life could cost him everything she knew he wanted. But she'd weighed the pros and cons and faced the truth: ending it now meant his dream could still come true.

The acknowledgment shattered her, and she felt her body tremble in protest. *Don't do it.* But she ignored the anxious flutter in her stomach. A clean break was best. Her heart banged out a last, desperate plea for safety. *Do. Not.*

Do. It.

"I'm sorry, Nick, but I want out. Not five weeks from now. Now." Marianne drew in a shaky breath. "Tonight."

"Tonight." Nick held his arms out wide, the daisies hanging in mid-air. "That's it? You say you're out and it's over?"

She tilted her chin in a defensive gesture. "I don't remember signing a contract."

"A contract? Jesus, I offered to draw something up, but you trusted me to be a man of my word." He barked out a laugh. "Guess I know why now."

Marianne heard the resentment in his voice and closed her eyes to edge back tears. When she opened them, he was still standing there, outwardly devastated, but impeccably controlled. The truth of what she'd done hit her hard. He believed her, and his distant, pained expression revealed another, even more difficult, truth. He'd never expected better. A stab of pain shot through her chest as the realization shattered her heart, tearing open old wounds so completely that she knew they'd never heal. She'd never recover from Nick Wright. And that was the most painful truth of all.

Marianne drew in one last shaky breath. "I'm sorry. But this deal is not going to work."

Nick remained frozen, and the distance between them filled with the kind of chill normally reserved for the worst days of a New York winter. Despite the spring blooms in his hand, a shiver raced down her spine. His face was etched in stone. And she knew it was over.

"These are for you." And then he turned on his heel, tossed the rain-splattered flowers onto the dusty, plastic-covered table, and walked out of her life for good.

Chapter Sixteen

"Always keep promises."
—mantelligence.com

Nick had never spent a sleepless night in his life.
Until tonight.

He sank back against the leather cushions. Guess he'd been right all along—commitment was for suckers. Marianne was gone. He'd been crazy to think their relationship was real, that it was different from any other he'd experienced. Relationships had never worked for him, so why had he expected more from her? Because she'd charmed him on his birthday by popping out of a damned cake? How insane was that?

Plain and simple—he'd been taken for a ride, and it was nuts to believe anything else. People left. That's what they did. Hell, everybody but his sister had left him in some way, and he'd dealt with it. So why was he sitting here cuddling up with the classic movie channel, missing his fiancée, believing he didn't have all the pieces of the puzzle? Why did he still think Marianne would be different? Because he did.

He clicked up the volume on the television to keep from dwelling on the way she'd filled the place with her romance novels and her cardigans. The way she'd captivated him with her intelligence and her trademark moves, her glasses and those killer legs.

His place wasn't the same without that damned woman in it. Worse, it might never be the same. The rooftop, the office, hell, the freaking shower. Marianne had breathed soul into the place. He muted the television and tossed the remote onto the couch. So much for his damned rules and his foolproof six-week plan. No back-to-back dates—out the window. No sleepovers—obviously he'd made a joke of that one. Thank God it wasn't football season or he'd be turning in his man card. He slunk deeper into the couch.

Marianne hadn't seemed like a con artist, a woman who'd play the game for what she wanted and take off. She'd seemed vulnerable and genuine and sincere.

Hell, he'd thought he loved her.

The black and white glow from the television illuminated the emptiness of the room. Quiet seeped around him. He missed the feeling that came with having her here. Missed the way she turned off every light in the place except the one she was using. The way she'd check on her damn Prius every day. The late-night movies and her insomnia. Missed the way her hips swayed and the way her eyes lit up at the sight of flowers. Missed taking her face in his hands and kissing her under the light of the city stars. The cardigans, the glasses… everything.

Son of a bitch. He didn't simply think he loved her. He *did* love her. Nick chuckled into the semi-darkness. He was in love with his fake fiancée. Strike that: ex-fake-fiancée. The knowledge came like a gavel slamming down on his heart, creating a pain so sharp that he fell deeper into the sectional wondering what had happened.

Nick knew from experience that not everybody got a shot at the real deal, and he wasn't about to waste his. As unlikely as it seemed, he was in love with sweet, sexy Marianne McBride. Now, there was only one question left. What was he going to do about it?

E arly the following morning, having driven the one hundred miles from Manhattan to East Hampton on three hours of sleep, Nick made the hard left past the sea grass, drove the Spider up the pebbled driveway, and parked under the cypress tree next to the house. Sometime last night, he'd decided to walk away from the firm, come here to set the legal record straight, and let the chips of his career fall where they may.

For better or worse, he loved Marianne in a way he'd never believed possible—with his entire heart—and he refused to accept that he was nothing more than a party date to her. If she didn't intend to explain her quick departure from his condo, then Nick needed to figure out what was going on and find a way to bring her back home. To his home. Where he wanted her. Where she belonged. The Hamptons seemed as good a place to start as any.

"Come on up, Nick." John McBride's deep, welcoming

voice called out from the upper deck of the oceanfront house. Resting back in an Adirondack chair, he waved him toward a hidden set of stairs at the end of the portico. "I've been waiting since you called."

Nick took the steps two at a time, reaching the deck in a few seconds. He was here to set the record straight about Marianne's ex, to do right by her father, and his gut told him there was no time to waste. "Thank you for agreeing to see me on such short notice, Mr. McBride."

"Call me John—we're about to become family," he said with a smile. "Besides, I should be thanking you for driving all the way out here given that my range of motion is being curtailed for the short-term." His smile turned into a smirk, and he lifted the leg of his khaki pants to reveal the ankle bracelet. "Coffee?" he asked, indicating the insulated white pot on a nearby glass table.

Nick accepted, grateful for the caffeine, but unsure if he was impressed or concerned by the man's easy acceptance of his house arrest. He took hold of the stoneware mug being pressed into his hands and sat on the edge of a second slatted chair. "John, if it works for you, I'll cut straight to the chase. A portfolio crossed my desk yesterday that creates a bit of an issue for me."

"You're concerned about the effect of my conviction on your career."

"No," Nick assured him quickly, his hands cutting into the air between them. "If I'm being honest, the issue had crossed my mind, but no, that's not why I'm here."

The older man's face settled into an inquiring, serious expression so reminiscent of his daughter's that Nick had to smile. "Long drive for a cup of coffee."

Nick's tired half smile acknowledged the statement. "Well, sir, the portfolio in question belongs to Jason Ward."

The man nodded astutely. "I see."

"He wanted to invest in a fund, so I reviewed his financials, and it looks to me like he made some well-timed profits, the kind that draw the attention of the SEC—am I in the ballpark here? Or am I spinning my wheels?"

John pulled off his readers and raised his eyebrows. "My wife was right about you. You are a smart one." He tossed his glasses next to a discarded newspaper on the table. "I didn't know they were illegal—not at first."

"Then why go down for it?"

There was a pause as he considered his answer. "Because I'm the one who gave him the tip. Not intentionally, of course, just a casual mention about the merger of a friend's company—stupid of me, really." He eased back in the chair, as comfortable as if he were telling a fairy tale. "Next thing I know, the SEC is knocking on the door looking for answers, and Jason is claiming he made the trade honestly, not knowing it wasn't public information. Named me as the tipster." He shook his head. "What was I going to do? Call my daughter's fiancé a liar? I *had* provided Jason with information."

"Makes sense to me," Nick said.

John chuckled and held out his upturned palms in a simple, eloquent gesture. "Hell, I *was* guilty. I failed to do my due diligence, trusted the wrong man, and the transaction was technically done under my watch."

"No offense, sir. But I'd think that Jason would know better than to act on inside information." Hell, he'd caught wind of "insider tips" a time or two. That didn't mean he'd ever acted on them.

"Yes, well…" Marianne's father drummed his fingers on the arm of the chair, his expression equal parts angry and indifferent. "Marianne was engaged to Jason. I'd have gutted my business to save her pain, so…" His words trailed off.

"So you gave him a pass and skipped an investigation."

"I had the insider information, and my company profited. So, yes, I made the deal with the Feds. No public mess or trial, an easier investigation. Everybody wins. Never considered the backlash to my daughter's career, but she always loved the numbers, not the money. Not sure she ever loved Jason, though, not after the way she handled him at the party the other night."

Nick leaned forward in his seat. "Yes, about that…"

"Keep your friends close and your enemies closer, right?" The older man winked and gestured toward the ankle monitor. "But I don't think we'll being seeing him around here anymore. Not now that Marianne is finished with him." He eased back into the chair and looked him square in the eye. "She loves you, Nick. Even an old fool like me can see that."

Nick shifted in his seat, uncertain a woman like Marianne could love him, but damn sure he loved her. "We could still go to the Feds, find a way to set the record right."

The older man smiled. "That means a lot to you—setting the record straight."

"Without a doubt." Nick looked over at him, ready to make his case. "My father was not a man to stand up for anyone or take the high road. Doing the right thing is important to me." *Especially when it came to Marianne.* He wanted to make sure nothing could hurt her—or their future—and he wanted to bring her home.

"Nick, from where I sit, you're nothing like your father, but there's nothing to set straight here, nobody to protect, because it's all water under the bridge. A short stint in prison was a small price to pay for what I believed was Marianne's happiness. No point looking back." He picked up his coffee and raised it in a toast. "Never a saint, I probably earned the time, anyway."

"But sir—"

"It's settled. Jason made plenty of legit profit working for me. Invest his money or send him packing, whatever works, but don't dredge up more pain or another scandal, let the past go," he said, definitively. "Just be good to my daughter."

"I will," Nick said, a small measure of hope seeping into his heart. "If she'll let me."

Chapter Seventeen

"I guess I wanted love more than anything else in the world."
—Marilyn Monroe

Marianne stared at the impossible matrix score. There must be some way to fine-tune the total. Her fingers flew across the screen. Perhaps it was a correlation issue. If she took the number of minutes she'd spent with Nick and divided them by the numbers of times he'd sent her mind and body reeling... She shook her head. No, obviously that was not going to work. Her fingers trembled above the keys.

She needed to find an adjustment to confirm her decision to break off their relationship, some confidence interval or standard deviation to prove the matrix was wrong about her and Nick. She wrinkled her nose at the screen. Hells bells, computer models predicted behavior all the time, not to mention explaining the occurrence of natural phenomena, hurricanes, earthquakes, so why not predict, or better yet, control love?

Their business deal had grown into passion and friendship. Yes, Nick had freed her inner siren and encouraged her sexuality, but she wasn't trying to get over the best sex ever—although sex with Nick *was* the best ever—no, she was trying to get over the one man she'd always love.

Drawing in a shaky breath, she snapped the cover of the tablet shut in one swift motion. No calculation could change her decision. Marianne wanted a lifetime of Nick Wright, but not if being with her cost him everything. She slid her hands beneath her glasses, pressed the heels of her palms against her eyes.

Statistically, only two percent of people suffered from broken heart syndrome, a small, but real, number. And she was among them. Glasses askew, her skirt wrinkled, her hair a mess, she was melting down in a way she never thought possible, and no Marilyn marathon could change the fact that her heart was completely shattered, literally aching from the pain. She'd agreed to a temporary engagement and committed the worst possible sin. She'd fallen *permanently* in love.

The click of Jane's heels against the tile caused her to smooth her skirt and straighten her glasses. No more sexy dresses. No more fishnets. No more scandalous shoes. Her inner siren's run was over. Back to plain, achingly serious Marianne.

Jane stopped in front of her desk, deposited a cup with the words GRANDE. PASSION. MARIANNE scrawled in black Sharpie across the front, and got straight to the point. "Nick was offered his partnership, but he turned it down."

Marianne eyed the paper cup as her splintered heart

started cautiously to collect its pieces. "Why?"

A sympathetic sound of impatience erupted from Jane's throat. "Because Nick is a good man with a heart of gold, okay? He's not just the guy whose serial relationships are always short-circuiting." She pushed the tea cup closer, and the words stared Marianne in the face. "But I think you already know that." She opened her mouth to object, but Jane waved her off. "Do you know he worked nights to get through college?" She shook her head. "Well, he did, and when he finally got a scholarship, he kept his night job to put Jake and me through school, too. Do not let go of this wonderful man, Marianne. Do. Not."

Marianne looked away, tears burning her eyes as she smoothed her wrinkled skirt. "He is wonderful, Jane—so, so wonderful, but our relationship only worked because it wasn't real, because of our deal. He never really wanted me. Not plain old regular new girl, Marianne. He wanted his cake girl for a temporary six weeks. No matter how wonderful he is, that hasn't changed."

Jane shook her head, obviously not buying it. "Nick was attracted to you from the minute he saw you pop out of that cake, yes, but somewhere along the line, he fell for you. For *Marianne*. Not the new girl or the cake girl, but for you. All of the wonderful, beautiful things that you are—inside and out." She sipped at her coffee and glanced at her over the rim of the cup. "And while we're on the subject of the cake girl, I *may* have a teeny-tiny confession." She tilted her head and tugged hard on her right ear, the childhood tell of a gambler's daughter. Cupid was about to lay all her cards on the table. "There never was an *actual* cake girl."

Marianne blinked behind the glasses, stunned, but

secretly thrilled by the revelation. "No cake girl?"

"No cake girl." A tight, forgive-me smile creased her face. "I arranged the cake for Nick's birthday, but not the girl, hoping that my favorite siren would climb in there and pop out in time to meet her statistically perfect match."

Marianne felt the heat spread across her cheeks. "So the dress…the shoes…"

"All on my Amex."

"Jane, honestly—"

Her hands flew into the air. "I know. I know, it was risky, but the look on your face when you saw him for the first time…and the way he smiled back at you…I mean, I *am* Cupid, right? So how could I resist when two people I love so…"

She was the original cake girl. *The only one for Nick.* The edges of her mouth curved into a half smile. "Oh, Jane." She jumped out of her chair and threw her arms around her friend's shoulders. "Statistically speaking, you're the smartest Cupid in town."

"Really?" she said, "You're not mad…"

"I'm not mad," she said, but Jane was already speaking over her.

"Because he loves you, Marianne. From what I can tell, he loves everything about you. But I think you already know that, too, which means the only real issue left is how do you intend to fix this? Because you are not going to throw away the best man who has ever happened to you."

Marianne picked up her cup and turned it around so that the words faced her friend. GRANDE. PASSION. MARIANNE. She smiled over at Jane, her eyes brimming. "You're right. I'm not."

Nick arrived home to find his ex-fiancée waiting in the hallway outside his condo, holding a picnic basket in one hand and a bottle of champagne in the other. She was dressed to kill in a preppy trench coat and a pair of ruby red stilettos, sexy proof that there was no place like home. Her usually perfectly pressed coat sported a few wrinkles, which made him wonder how long she'd been waiting. He hoped not too long, although he knew he'd wait for her forever.

Goddamn, how he loved her.

He approached the door, stood across from her, and waited to hear the words he knew would change his life forever. Because he was ready. Nick was done with the rules. He wanted to take this woman out on back-to-back dates. He wanted to share sleepovers every Sunday during football season. No, every night. Every night for the rest of his life.

Her unwavering blue eyes caught his. "Are you sure about passing on the partnership?"

Nick nodded, knowing he'd never been more certain of any decision he'd ever made. "I'm sure."

"No regrets?"

"No regrets." He reached out to straighten the collar of her trench. "Not if I have you."

"Well, then, counselor." She dropped her chin and glanced up at him from behind her glasses. "You're in luck, because I've consulted with the 'legal department' at Smart Cupid…"

"The 'legal department'?" He leaned his hip against the doorjamb.

Marianne nodded and kept on talking. "Apparently, the whole 'fake engagement' portion of our agreement is totally unenforceable in a court of law."

"Really?" he said.

"*Totally* unenforceable," she said, with a teasing gleam in her eyes, "*Love*, however, is a different story, love is totally binding." She tilted her head back and looked up at him, tracing the line of buttons on his shirt with the champagne bottle. "And according to my most recent matrix calculation, after analyzing all the data, I have determined that you love me."

She bit down on her bottom lip and waited for confirmation.

Down the hallway, the elevator dinged as a smile inched across his face. He took the sapphire and diamond engagement ring out of his pocket. "Marry me?"

Returning his smile with one of her own, Marianne swayed another inch closer. "Did I mention I'm naked underneath this trench?"

He cocked an eyebrow. "Can I take that as a legally binding 'yes'?"

"Yes." Her whispered answer sent his heart soaring as every piece of the puzzle fell perfectly into place. "Absolutely, yes."

Nick brushed a kiss across her lips and slipped the ring back onto her finger where it belonged. "I love you."

"I love you, too." Marianne dropped the picnic basket and wrapped her arms around his shoulders, the champagne bottle hard against his back.

Nick gathered her against his chest and pulled them into the doorframe. He planned to tell her about her ex and his conversation with her dad…everything, so that there would never be any secrets between them. He wanted to know why she'd packed up and left, too. But she was here now—home. The rest of the truth could wait until the morning. Until he proved to her how much he loved her—body and soul. Then he'd let go of the past and embrace a permanent future with his anything-but-temporary fiancée.

A future he hoped would last forever.

"Think we'll make it?" he asked.

She smiled up at him, a mischievous twinkle at the back of her blue eyes. "Statistically speaking, I'm 99 percent sure."

He tilted his head back and laughed up at the ceiling, happier than he'd ever been, more sure of his commitment to her than of anything he'd ever done. "And the other one percent?"

Eyes never leaving his, Marianne took a step back as her hands dropped to the belt at her waist. She untied the knot and let her coat fall away. "Convince me."

Epilogue

White and blue twinkle lights reflected against the white canopied tent, and Marianne smiled up at Nick, loving her newly minted husband in his conservative tux and sexy, undone tie. Her voice softened with a hint of wonder. "We did it."

The band played Ed Sheeran's "Kiss Me," and Nick twirled her around the edge of the parquet dance floor. "You're stuck with me now."

"For six weeks?"

"For sixty years," he said, a look of pure love etched across his handsome face.

A few feet away on a round table covered in white linen

sat a three-tiered wedding cake, a custom-made replica of her husband's birthday cake, complete with a raised pop-out top and a dark-haired groom embracing a bride clad in a silver-sequined dress. On the second tier, nestled under the Brooklyn Bridge, a cupid sat mischievously aiming her arrow up at the unsuspecting couple. The cake was a gift from Jane and Charlie, a sly reminder of how a siren got her man.

With her hand clasped in his, Nick led her off the dance floor and into a corner of the canopy that had been set up on the lawn of her parents' property. Moonlight streamed at the edges mixing in with the twinkle lights to create a romantic atmosphere that would make even Martha Stewart proud. Pre- or post-parole.

Only three weeks until Nick had to be back at Morgan Wealth Management & Trust. Once the dust settled from the scandal, Dan Morgan came to see Nick's exemplary honesty and his commitment to Marianne as something positive, offered him a short leave of absence, and put off the partner decision for six months, the implication clear that the firm wanted him to have it once the smoke cleared.

After she'd revealed how Drew had blackmailed her into giving up Nick, he'd been scolded by Dan, since airing such *less-than-squeaky-clean* laundry could've negatively impacted the firm. An excellent result from her standpoint and, best of all, there were no secrets between them. Now they had twenty-one days, seven hours and approximately thirty-five minutes left to enjoy their honeymoon, and Marianne intended to make the most of every second.

Nick drew her into his arms and brushed a kiss across her lips. "About time to leave, Mrs. Wright," Nick said, adjusting her glasses against the bridge of her nose. "Are you ready?"

"One more minute." Her eyes filled with tears as she glanced around the beachside tent full of her friends and family. Dad held her mom in his arms as she gazed up at him, laughing alongside her father's parole officer, who looked pretty cozy with Nick's mom. Across the room, Dan showed off a few card tricks, clearly determined to take Marianne for a pretty penny at the firm's next casino night. Cupid and her man, Charlie, huddled together in a sexy clinch at their table, and while her new brother-in-law hadn't been able to make it to the States for the party, he'd sent a case of champagne and a copy of his book on love. Not that they'd need it. Like the matrix said, they shared a forever kind of love. Nothing *temporary* about it.

Marianne had been a quiet, lonely kid, her head full of computer code and numbers, but no statistical equation could explain the joy she felt tonight surrounded by a wide circle of friends and family. She smiled over at Nick, happier than she'd thought possible. "Ready, Mr. Wright."

Nick nodded and, across the makeshift room, the band announced the departure of the bride and groom, bursting into their version of Coldplay's "A Sky Full of Stars." As the music filled the night air, Nick pulled her into a swift, passionate kiss before grabbing her hand to race through the gathering crowd of friends and family.

Confetti rained down on them, and she turned to blow her parents a kiss. A lump in her throat, she lifted her Marilyn-inspired, satin Vera Wang gown to climb into the Alfa Romeo and her ruby red heels sparkled in the moonlight. As the happy cheers continued from the edges of the tent, Marianne settled into the car beside her husband. *Her husband.* How she loved the sound of those words.

Nick chuckled at the handwritten sign, anchored to the back of the car, SMART CUPID APPROVED. Eyes filling, he turned to give his sister one last wave before settling into the driver's seat. "Think we should break the speed limit?" he asked. "Just this once?"

Marianne smiled over at him. "If it means starting the honeymoon sooner…"

Nick waggled his eyebrows, revved the convertible's engine, and took off down the pebbled driveway toward Ocean Avenue. Marianne looked up at the star-studded sky, but she didn't have one wish. Behind them, a collection of tin cans clanked against the road, and a dozen heart-shaped balloons reached toward the heavens, as they raced toward what Marianne knew would be life's greatest adventure—love.

Acknowledgments

Once upon a time, in a faraway land called the 'Burgh, a hapless author got lucky. No, not that kind of lucky—rather, she was fortunate enough to connect with a talented editor whose cool is unsurpassed. And so, my endless thanks to Vanessa Mitchell, fab editor and awesome chick. Your ideas and encouragement spur my imagination, and your patient feedback keeps me on track when I'd veer off course. I thank my lucky stars for you.

Big thanks also to Elley Arden, and fellow Entangled authors, Robin Bielman and Samanthe Beck for diving into the first draft of this story with big hearts. *Unexpectedly His* is better because of you. I only aspire to one day rise to the level of your crazy talents.

A special thank you to Kyle of mantelligence.com for allowing me to freely quote his masculine wisdom and for being my go-to source for all things manly. You are adored.

It's funny, but one of my favorite aspects of the first two

Smart Cupid books is the friendship between Marianne and Jane. I love how they support and challenge and encourage and frustrate, but ultimately love, one another. Melissa Smith-Beckner, my BFF of thirty-seven years, thank you—for the inspiration, for everything. And finally, to Micah, my first and oldest bestie, my longtime supporter, I love you.

Lastly, thank you to my husband and two little boys for still recognizing me when I stumble up from the basement, unshowered and bleary-eyed and looking for pizza. There's no one I love more in the world.

About the Author

After ten years of survival, aka working, in Hollywood, this former actress and current author of sexy contemporary romance is living happily-ever-after in Pittsburgh with her longtime sweetie, AKA Husband Number 1, and their two punky kids. When not carpooling to birthday parties or testing her gourmet cooking skills by throwing a frozen pizza into the oven, Maggie daydreams about sneaking off to Vegas or Napa, or even just the movies. A love of red wine, Italian food, and music round out her list of life's greatest joys. Oh, and Tuesday night karaoke, totally underrated fun.

Discover the **Smart Cupid** *series...*

BREAKING THE BACHELOR

Matchmaker Jane Wright just made a bet—she'll find the "perfect" match for Manhattan's hottest confirmed bachelor, sexy-as-sin bartender Charlie Goodman—Jane's ex-lover—or lose her company. Charlie doesn't want to see Jane's business fail. He just wants a little revenge. Determined to prove that chemistry *always* beats compatibility algorithms, he plans to drive Jane crazy with desire, then walk away. And Charlie's plan is working.